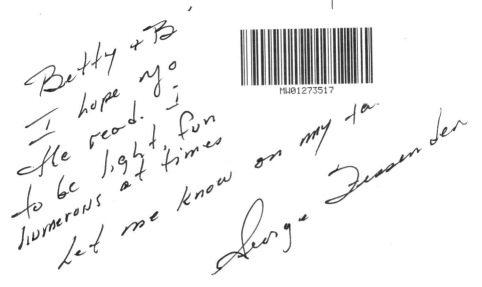

Betty + B'
I hope yo
the read. I
to be light, fun
humerous at times
Let me know on my ta-
George Fessenden

FOR THE GOOD OF ALL

George Fessenden

Raider Publishing International

New York   London   Johannesburg

First Printing

ISBN: 1-935383-62-0
Published By Raider Publishing International
www.RaiderPublishing.com
New York London Johannesburg

Printed in the United States of America and the United Kingdom

PRAISE FOR...
Acknowledgements

Margaret Ann Fessenden, my wife, stood by me throughout the writing of this book, often looking at me, stating, "You're here in the here and now, but you're not really here with me. You are vacant. You are deep somewhere in your book." Margaret understood what I was going through, as she was a counselor and understood me when many would have otherwise thought that I had simply lost my marbles. I can't thank Margaret enough for her brutal honesty when it came to conducting the first editing of this book, and I still smile over her comment to me. "Scrap Chapter Two. Start over. This chapter has no relevance." We are still so much in love.

Allan Speevak, a good friend and an exceptionally creative professional photographer of Peninsula Photography, White Rock, British Columbia, Canada, transformed my verbal version of the book's cover into a fine object of art. Many thanks, Al, for your wonderful creation.

Tom Carson, Raider, Publishing International Editor, your frank comments, while hard hitting and humbling at times were much appreciated, as they served my best interests in improving the overall read of the book. Some of your comments presented a great challenge for me in filling in the gaps that I had left and again were very important in improving the dialogue. I had to smile to myself when Tom said, "Scrap Chapter 2, the rewritten version." Chapter 2 was deleted and Chapter 3 is now Chapter 2, and so on.

DEDICATION

To *Donald Guy Fessenden,* a hard-working, well-principled, loving and giving, dedicated family man whom I lost all too early in life. You are a big part of my life today. I love you, and by the way, I never thanked you for the natural gifts that you passed on to me; life is great.

And to *Margaret Ann Fessenden (Ryan),* my adorable, loving, hard-working wife, best friend, and lover. You're the only person in this world that I can talk with, confide in, and be vulnerable with. You let me be me and have helped me immensely with self-speak and being comfortable with my emotional inside. I love you and thank you for always being there for me. You're my "Digby Chick".

FOR THE GOOD OF ALL

George G. Fessenden

BHGDATNIOEEDTTHENRWSRHREDTL
ALAEIYAUDREGIOWYEOEEORTIRNR
OPNESLWEDFAIXALLWETNNPSOEWR

CONTENTS

PROLOGUE

The world is ever in a state of change, is change for the betterment of its civilization and...?

Greed, lust, and treachery have been witnessed since before Christ; is it more or less in shaping the World we live in today?

The economic engines driving humankind have changed over the centuries; what benefits or threats result in its power and obsessions?

The human being is considered the most complex and evolved of all species created; is this evolution optimized and complete?

Have morals and values evolved or eroded, and are they in sync with the times?

Have you felt the presence of something that isn't or perhaps is?

The World is at a crossroads; its sensitive environment and fragile life supporting balance is in competition with all the human motivations; what might the outcome be?

CHAPTER 1
Odd Ordeal

Jake and Maggie walk their most prized golden retriever Katey on East Beach all year round, given the relatively mild weather experienced on the West Coast in and around Semiahmoo Bay. Besides, what better place is there for a retriever than the beach— chasing after a ball, socializing with all her pals, and just plain getting wet so that she can treat her owners to an oh so refreshing cooling spray as she shakes off the excess water with pride and certain intention.

On this particular August afternoon, August 15, 2006, to be precise, with temperatures hovering in the low eighties, Jake suggests to Maggie that a walk on the beach would bring some relief from the heat and refresh their energy for a more productive and rewarding afternoon of fun. Maggie was hoping Jake would suggest a nice romantic stroll on the beach and quickly responds, "I would love to take a walk on the beach today, Jake, but in this heat, Katey would simply expire".

"I wasn't thinking of taking Katey today, darling. It's too hot for her, so let's make this stroll romantic. After all it's our turn; don't you think?"

After just a quick ten-minute walk, they arrive on East Beach and inhale the rhapsody of the wonderful ocean air.

Maggie can never quite get enough of the salty and sassy aroma wafting from the ocean air and thus frequents the bay as often as time will permit.

"It's so peaceful and serene here, Jake, listening to the magical roar of the ocean, watching and listening to the birds sing and frolic in the air; oh look, Jake, how majestic! Two immature bald eagles spiraling toward the ocean waters, spinning and twisting end-over-end with their talons interlaced together in free fall— just like a couple of kids being kids, playing around," Maggie states with awe swimming through her ruffled mind.

"Maggie, this beach is heavenly, and it means the world to me as well. It is the one place where I can clean the myriad of dust-doomed cob webs from my head; it has to do with the aromatic air and the sounds of the ocean roar that cascade through one ear and out the other, cleansing and scrubbing the stale amass away."

"Jake, I can never get over just how beautiful the snow-white-capped peak of Mount Baker looks and the fact that the snow remains all year round, yet it is ever so close to the ocean. I feel like I can just reach out and touch it, as it dominantly fills the landscape with such regal beauty and dominance."

"My thoughts are with you, Maggie, and when encapsulating the gulf islands and the West Coast Mountains, this area is truly beyond belief."

The ocean usually exhibits a bit of a tainted brown, sometimes pea green hue, given its proximity to such a substantial urban metropolis, but today, it glistens brightly in the intense sunlight, its luster unusually deep blue in color, and it lays perfectly placid.

"I don't know why, but I just can't help repeating myself. I never cease to be amazed at the ever-lasting beauty which proliferate this region by the sea. I feel so calm and am at great peace here; this must be our paradise."

"It is, Maggie, a near perfect and complete picture of our paradise that I wish to live my life out in. I love you, Maggie, so deeply more every day."

"I love you, too, Jake. You mean everything to me; I feel so lucky and blessed at this time of my life to have you in my life".

"That's a ditto, Babe," Jake says with a proud broad

grin."

"Jake, what did you mean by 'a near perfect picture'?"

"Katey isn't with us today; otherwise, it would be perfect."

Only minutes later, Maggie leaps back and gasps, as she spies a pale green vog or fog shimmering over the waters of Semiahmoo Bay, lifting, turning, heaving, and swirling around, but ironically, its movements appears to be in tune to a Viennese waltz. It is truly an odd thing of immense beauty exhibiting such gracefulness. It is titillating to watch, and frankly, they are both in awe, spellbound at the sight of something so unearthly in nature. While they have experienced vog in Hawaii in their past, never have they encountered anything quite so romantically menacing like this before, and never have they encountered anything like it in the media or topics written by the Science World at large. Then, science isn't their forte, so it is entirely possible that they could have missed something on this topic.

Abruptly, its movements distort, becoming odd and unpredictable, rattling, then cascading across the glassy bay with rancorous ferociousness. One thing's for sure, it is moving with keen intent toward them.

"I don't know what to make of it, Maggie."

"What is it, Jake?"

"It's so strangely eerie, so contiguous, Maggie. I just don't know yet."

"Jesus, it's not just a cloud, Jake. It's hot, humid, and lavender-smelling. It's scarring the crap out of me," Maggie says, as she holds Jake dearly for some warm and reassuring comfort!

"An odd, tumultuous overture" Jake muses.

While basic instinct suggests that they should run, they are literally frozen in place by the sheer uniqueness of this ominous entity appearing before their curious eyes. Perhaps you could say that they are in some hypnotic state of disbelief. This bizarre, greenish cloud now appears to metastasize with ferocity, creating massive curling, inverted waves, crashing like something you might see on the North Shore of Oahu, huge breakers swirling with oscillating turbulence and force. This thing is now exhibiting a full green color spectrum to the pure ivory white at its crest. Closer and closer the vog or fog came, triggering its pre-winds, hurling sand in their faces, flattening their hair, and compelling them into a bent-over deportment, struggling not only to stand but to understand.

Desperate to move and so solidly frozen in place, they concede, colliding with its onslaught. With disquieting fury, the vog or fog consumes them; they vanished off the East Beach and into a somewhat heavenly space without definitive description.

CHAPTER 2
Stunned

Jake and Maggie, suddenly realizing they're once again standing on East Beach, are stunned in utter disbelief. "Maggie!" Jake exclaimed. "What the fuck happened?" Nothing more could emanate from Jake's mouth at that moment as he was nearing delirium.

Maggie, distraught, agog, and fraught with confusing fear, yet regurgitating inner mystical feelings, couldn't vocalize. Shaking violently, her sweaty hands covering her mouth, standing there frozen, squinting with pure amazement, still agape, points to where the green vog or fog was or where she thinks that is was… She isn't sure. She is very much perplexed, disoriented, and bewildered yet somewhere profoundly within, she feels warmth and joy.

A lingering, nerve-racking minute or two pass before Maggie regains sufficient composure, then abruptly blurts out in a perfectly, painfully horrid, squeaky utterance, "FOR THE GOOD OF ALL. FOR THE GOOD OF ALL. FOR THE GOOD OF ALL."

"Maggie!" Jake cries out. "I think you're right. I can't confirm, but somehow that sounds vaguely familiar. I am at a loss, too. I know. I think something happened and 'FOR THE GOOD OF ALL' is somehow ringing through. We need to get home now, Maggie. This is all too weird, what we have just been put through and the strange feelings that exist. I am having difficulties coping. I don't know why this happened; it's a mystery! My head is spinning like a top and oh, my eyes are sore. For mercy's sake alive, they are really sore. Hurry, Maggie. Oh my God, Maggie, this is

7

way too much; my mind is a complete and total wreck. I think I need a drink. Perhaps a stiff scotch, maybe two, will do something to help the pain of it all go away."

"I'm with you, Jake. Don't leave without me. Right now, my head is just swimming with monkey mind stuff that doesn't make sense. My eyes are incredibly sore, too. I'm hungry, and I am also worried about Katey girl."

Holding hands, giving each other gentle hugs and comforting encouragement, their homeward journey feels to them like a trek and a half. They did not realize the colossal expenditure of energy consumed during their out-of-this-world, mysterious escapade! Nearly exhausted to the brink of collapse, staggering and swaggering, they head for home.

Approaching home, their recollection of the beach event is no more lucid now than when they were standing distraught on the beach. Their dumbfounded disorientation lingers on, leaving them somewhat helpless, but this persistent thought of warmth and joy still simmers in the dimly lit portion of their sub-consciences.

Their excited neighbor, Dave, noticing them walking ever so slowly down the sidewalk, waves with panic on his face, stating, "We have been worried about you guys! Where have you been? Katey's been howling non-stop, and scratching like a bitch in heat, to get out. She's been frantic. Man oh man, she has been frantic with total fear in her face. I didn't have your key; otherwise, I would have let her out."

Maggie calmly says, "I don't understand, Dave. We just..." and then goes into hysterics, just being reminded about Katey, and races to the front door.

Katey is frenzied and spinning out of control, for the need to get out, for the joy of seeing them, or just scared of being left alone. Who knows? As Maggie frantically unlocks and opens the front door, Katey leaps through it, clearing the staircase with the greatest of ease and bee-lines it straight for the end of the garage. Then, she side slips around the garage and screeches to a halt, giving

Jake a warm look. Satisfying herself that Jake is actually there, she decides she cannot wait any longer and quickly marches out onto the lawn to release the painful discomfort that had built up within her."

"Dave, I just cannot understand why Katey is being so agitated. It's highly unusual for her. Maggie and I have only been gone about a half-hour or forty-five minutes and..."

"A half an hour?" Dave exclaims. "Give your head a shake man! It's been THREE DAYS— like seventy-two hours. Shouldn't we be just a little bit concerned about your welfare or what?"

You can hear a pin drop, and a pale, ashen look appears on Jake and Maggie's faces. Their blood is seemingly gushing to the soles of their feet as life is being sucked right out of them.

"What day is it?" Maggie asks in a somewhat subdued a dumbfounded manner?

"Tuesday", Dave replies.

With that response, Maggie faints.

"Jesus H. Christ, Dave. I don't believe it. Help me with Maggie, Dave; I've got to get her in the house and quick."

Laying Maggie on the sofa in the family room, Jake quickly dampens a hand towel, and gently places it on her forehead. Maggie slowly starts to recover from her near catatonic state and just stares blindly, trying to fathom and confirm just what is going on. A wee hint of color gradually appears on her face. It sure wouldn't take a psychologist long to understand that something has really gone off the rails in Maggie's mind.

"I - I - I believe you, Dave, or at least I'm trying to believe you," Maggie blurts out,

"Jake, please turn on the TV to confirm, to verify or provide anything— proof— before I go nuts. I need to know what day this really is. I need a drink. Oh Sweetie, can you get me a glass of white wine— not that garage bingo stuff, but a good, store bought Sauvignon Blanc."

"Coming right up, Babe, and I think I'm going to have a double scotch, neat, a good single malt, I might add. Perhaps I will make it MacCallans seventeen-year, cask strength. Dave, do you want a beer?"

"No thanks, Jake. I think I had better get home. You guys obviously need time alone to get a grip on what's going on in your lives right now. You guys are too far out for me. I'm out of here."

Katey can't quite seem to get enough of their attention, so, as usual, she wedges in between them at the kitchen bar and gives them a nudge when she thinks they are being remiss. A guess would have it that the way that they are feeling about now has given them little want to dote on the Katey. They are way too far into their own heads to even notice their beloved dog. The queen of the household is in dire need of a good pat. Soon she is fast asleep at their feet, with one eye open to be sure, listening in on their strange conversation.

"You know, Maggie, I have been sitting here thinking about what happened to us, and, you know, it's still a virtual blank, a blank spot in my memory banks. There is, however, one thing I have noticed, and, Sweetie, it ain't the scotch talking. I know that I've only had two, maybe three well-deserved ones, but I'm telling ya my eyes have come back to 20/20. Look at this: no glasses and I can actually read the regular print in the newspaper. I can see that the time on your watch is 9:30 P.M. Hey! No struggle, strain, or pain and no glasses. This is unbelievable, and frankly, I can't help thinking it is linked to what happened to us this afternoon. Wouldn't it be fantastic if we have been spirited through the Fountain of Youth? I wouldn't mind getting a little younger, if you catch my drift. What do you think, Darling?"

"I don't think, I don't know, and I don't care at this moment, my darling Jake. I'm too tired and just want to go to bed."

CHAPTER 3
Black Out

Global Protector, or more commonly referred to as
the "Eagle", is responsible for the U.S. Worldwide Satellite
Communication and Visual Ground Surveillance Network.
Tremendous monitoring capabilities exist within this
network that oversees "the eyes and ears of Uncle Sam's"
worldwide activities. As an example, troop movement in
Afghanistan can be followed. The power of the satellite's
telescope's multiple-layered lenses provide for exact details
of such movement, like the number of troops and the
precise types and number of armament vehicles, and the
Eagle assists the military and their generals in developing
their war-games strategy and in locating the enemy. It can
also estimate with pinpoint accuracy the timing of
engagement based on the speed of the troop movement and
the distance to the insurgents and the anticipated terrain
obstacles.

The Eagle listens in on communications being
transmitted globally and, more specifically, can zero in to
any area of the world should the U.S. suspect or identify a
security breach or just decide to carry out general
surveillance for the good of the nation. To be "number
one", you have to keep an eye and ear on everything above,
below, and on this vast planet called Earth. This network of
satellites has been built-up over the years to ensure no
ground space is ever out of view. The oceans are well-
covered, meaning ongoing movement of all ships large and
small is being tracked. An undersea capability is currently
being developed, which will give observers a complete
scan of the ocean to the depth of one thousand fathoms or

11

more. Authorities are somewhat mum on the potential capabilities, all for the security of the nation.

An extremely powerful network, the Eagle is working 24/7 to ensure the security of the nation. The Eagle is directly linked to the NSA (National Security Agency) as a cooperating arm, with ties to the World Wide Web Internet within its reach.

On August 18, at precisely 1:30 PM (EDT), Captain Harold Willis of the Eagle's Middle Eastern monitoring section, Alfa Satellite Network 1-22 notices blurring distortions on Alpha 13. At first, intermittent, wavy lines are racing across the monitoring screens. Captain Willis immediately summons Major Hall. This oddity catches his interest, and Major Hall begins adjusting the vertical and horizontal settings to improve the images, but to no avail. Within a minute, maybe two, the distortion becomes so severe that no intelligent information can be retrieved. The monitoring screen simply blacks out.

Major Hall calls Colonel Britch. He stated, "We have a major glitch with Alpha 13. This satellite is effectively non-functional, as it has blacked out I request your take on this, sir. I have ordered up the best technical team to assist us."

"Major," Colonel Britch replies, "this means we have a surveillance gap in Iran."

"Yes, it appears that we have a twenty minute gap in not only Iran, but the other countries; Alpha 13 is the eyes and ears over in its orbit."

"This is serious... deadly serious," Colonel Britch replies. "What's the status of Alpha 14 and 15, Major?"

"Sir, Alpha 14 and 15 are functioning as expected, sir."

"Okay, good. We need to be sure there are no other glitches in the Alpha operating system. As well, check with your counterparts on the operations of the other worldwide satellites systems to determine their security level. As soon as I apprise General Whitmore, I'll be at your door."

"I'm on to it, sir."

"Whitmore here."

"Sir, this is Britch. A serious breach of security currently exists over Iran. The Alpha 13 satellite is non-functional as we speak. Major Hall is handling the situation now and has the best technical assistance to assist in assessing the situation. Sir, we need to alert Homeland Security and the president".

"I'm on it, Britch. Keep me updated."

The Alpha 13 monitoring screen slowly starts to develop a few wavy lines, static, and blurring images as Alpha 13 starts to correct itself. Within a minute or two, Alpha 13 once again becomes fully functional on the monitor.

There is major jubilance in the Eagle's Nest. The cheers can be heard throughout the center, and only one thing can possibly be on the minds of those within earshot: It is a return for Alpha 13. Everyone congregates around Alpha 13's monitor to share in the moment of glory with smiles and handshakes. This sort of thing has never happened in the past, and while it appears to be a temporary glitch, Major Hall isn't buying into that theory.

"We can't assume anything in this business," the Major states, "so the continued deployment of the technical team is necessary to ensure the source of the glitch is found and confirmed. The risks are too high not to go the extra mile when it comes to national security.

"Major Hall here. Colonel Britch, Alpha 13's screen returned to normal, sir. We are currently all focusing our attention on trying to identify what went wrong. I am continuing the deployment of the technical team until we are satisfied we have the situation under control. Colonel, as we have no idea what happened, I have requested the technical team look into the possibility of getting a visual of Alpha 13. Technical is now in the process of maneuvering Alpha 16 into a new orbit so we can observe Alpha 13."

"Good work, Major, keep me posted"

"Major Hall, sir," Captain Willis yells out, "the monitoring screen of Alpha 15 just blacked out."

"That can't be," Major Hall blurts out.

"At what precise moment did this black out occur?"

"14:20, sir."

"All eyes are requested on Alpha 13, 14, and 15 monitor screens. We seem to have an unknown problem on our hands affecting the satellites over Iran," states Major Hall. "Any deviation from the expected operations must be reported to me immediately.

"Colonel Britch, Major Hall here. Alpha 15 has now blacked out. Sir, this may be coincidental, or it may be an indicator of a larger issue. I have instructed all eyes on the monitors of Alpha 13, 14, and 15 to determine if a pattern can be supported."

"Major, what about Alpha 14?"

"Alpha 14 is functioning as expected, sir. Admittedly, we did have a lapse in monitoring the screens when Alpha 13 began functioning again. We were so elated and relieved to have Alpha 13 functioning as normal again, we temporally left our posts. Part of our monitoring now is to determine any further black outs."

"Okay Major, I will sit on this one for thirty minutes before I go upstairs with the bad news. Keep me posted."

At precisely 14:40, or 2:40 P.M., Alpha 13 starts developing distortion and static in its imaging, and within a minute or two, the monitoring screen blacks out again. Alpha 15, at the same time, is reported to be in the recovery process. As wavy lines appear on its monitor, static cracks and the visual is once again restored.

"Colonel Britch, Major Hall here. Alpha 13 has again blacked out, and Alpha 15 has now restored itself. We are beginning to believe we have some form of interference over Iran; however, we cannot confirm that for another nineteen minutes. If Alpha 14 blacks out, then we definitely have a larger problem. I will keep you posted... Colonel Britch, sir, in regards to my counterparts

14

experiencing any difficulties with their satellite systems, that would be a negative, sir."

"Hmm, it is oddly strange. Keep your focus on our issues."

"Yes, sir".

"Major Hall, General Whitmore here. Patch me over to Colonel Britch."

"General Whitmore, Britch here."

"All parties are briefed to the situation. The president requires an update every twenty minutes. You are charged with that responsibly, Colonel. Use the red phone. The president is mustering up us, along with the Joint Chiefs of Staff, the NSA, and Homeland Security."

"General, there have been additional developments," Colonel Britch states.

"There appears to be some form of interference over Iran affecting the operations of our satellites. Alpha 13 and 15 have both blacked out over Iran and then have resumed operations outside of Iran's air space. In about thirteen minutes, we will have the information regarding Alpha 14."

"Okay", General Whitmore states. "We will wait for the results prior to further advising the president."

"Major Hall, be advised that our level of security is now Orange alert."

"Yes, sir, Colonel."

CHAPTER 4
Encounter

Maggie is restless, not able to get the recent events off her mind. She cannot understand how different she feels from a few days ago. The scary part of it all is that there are no apparent answers, except that she knows what she knows. It did happen, for what reason: all unexplained. She tosses and turns for an hour or so and then slowly drifts into a light restless state of sleep. Maggie's mind starts working in nearly over-heated overdrive. She starts dreaming.

Her dreams usually represent the good and fun times in her life, the serendipitous life she leads with Jake, the wonderful memories of her once young children, who are now grown men— acknowledging her enjoyment of those great picnics and bon-fires she has attended on the beach, going on hikes in the mountains were awe inspiring, sitting with Jake, having endless hours of good, solid discussions, planning and keeping up with each others' interests, fears, and accomplishments, and, of course, Katey, being a current central figure in her activities. What is life without being able to reminisce a favorable past through a medium such as dreaming.

Then, without warning, her dreams take on a different theme, and she screams and writhes beneath the sheets. Maggie seems to be in a sheer panicky state for hours but, in reality, it is only seconds. Jake awakens and begins shaking her to bring her out of the hysteria she is in.

"Maggie, Maggie, wake up. Wake up, Baby, are you okay or what?"

Maggie, dripping sweat from her brow and panting

hard in a nearly uncontrollable state states, "I don't know, Jake. I'm scared, damn good and scared."

"Scared of what, Maggie?" Jake says.

"I was having a terrible dream, but damn it all anyway. I can't remember a thing. It was so scary. It's a blank, such a complete blank."

"It's 1:00 a.m. Oh Maggie, I know this dream is upsetting, but Sweetie, we simply have to get some rest and well-deserved sleep. We need to be sharp so we can figure things out in the morning. Things are confusing for me as well, Maggie. I just can't seem to understand anything anymore. Maybe you should just hold me in your thoughts until you go to sleep, Babe. Slide over a little bit, honey, I think a gentle cuddle will likely take your mind off recent events."

"Oh! I love you so much, Jake. Thanks for being here with me."

"It's definitely my pleasure, Babe."

At 6:00 a.m., Maggie wakes up with a smile on her face and gives Jake a warm kiss on his cheek. Jake awakens and says, "That was wonderful; do it again." Well, one thing led to another, and love made in Heaven naturally and blissfully overtook them.

Feeling somewhat drained Maggie, with a coy smile on her face, says, "Jake, I met your father last night."

"You did what!" Jake said.

"Shush! Don't spoil my vividly awesome memory of my first impressions of your father. Oh, what a wonderful time we had. Your father was most pleased to finally meet me, and he did admit from his viewing port that you made a good catch, Jake."

"He's got that right, Maggie," Jake chuckles."

"He couldn't wait to tell me things about when you were a little boy and how much he wished he had been more patient with you. He really couldn't understand how you could ever accomplish anything given the fact you were left-handed. You apparently looked so clumsy every time you undertook anything, especially when working

17

with your hands. He said you were always eager to help, and he would have to stop and think: 'Oh, God, give me the gift of patience.' One time, he said, with a loving smile, that while you were helping repair the guard railing above the basement steps, you actually damaged the new rail beyond repair attempting to hammer in the nails. We laughed, and I remembered you had told me that story, too."

"Well Maggie," Jake says, "I may have been clumsy and awkward, and I may have taken my share of humiliation, but at least I always operated in my right mind. I am much better off today for my struggles of yesterday. I am totally ambidextrous and damn proud of it."

"Do you want to see your dad, Jake? He would like to see you."

"I would love to see my dad, Maggie. I have yearned for it so long, Sweetie, but he has been dead for thirty-three years. Ah, you were dreaming, Maggie, just dreaming. Don't diddle with me."

"No, No, No, get dressed. Hurry. We are going to see your father."

"How do we accomplish that, Maggie?"

"You just go get yourself dressed, and you will see... Are you ready, Jake?"

"You're serious aren't you?"

"Yes!"

"Then lead the way, Babe. I'll play into your game."

"It's not far. Hold my hand. We are only a step away."

Maggie and Jake slip through an invisible portal into a parallel universe.

"Oh my god, Maggie, is this ever an idyllic place! I'm simply stunned beyond belief. Just hang on a minute while my eyes absorb all this. Wow this is how I had always pictured Heaven— a beautiful lake, every kind of bird you would ever want to see, magnificent trees, colossal mountains, flowers of every kind in ample abundance. This

18

place is so lovely and warm and as picturesque as Michelangelo's paintings in the Sistine Chapel. Look, Maggie: many happy faces appearing perfectly content with their paradise. Its' really strange; the locals don't seem to acknowledge our presence? Where's Dad, Maggie?"

"Just be patient. He will come when he is ready."

"Is this Heaven? Are we still alive?"

"Are we still alive, Jake? I was here last night. Don't you remember?"

Walking across a beautifully manicured, lush, emerald green lawn expanse, Jake stops in his tracks and stares in disbelief. His father is approaching.

"Dad, is that... it's really you," Jake says and throws his arms around him, and his father returns the warm reunion. With tears rolling out of his eyes, Jake is so filled with emotional excitement, as he hasn't seen him in thirty-three years. The painful memories that Jake has held quickly come back, as he did not anticipate his dad's departure on that fateful day and was not able to be there for his last moments.

"Dad, you seem to be yourself as I remember you. Your warm, and you appear full of life. Why aren't you with us on Earth?"

"Son, my appearances are such not to frighten you. I am not what I seem, and I can no longer exist on your Earth, as I have moved beyond and now serve the Higher Power. My home is here and here is what we call Meadowbrook. Meadowbrook is a pristine bucolic place, complete with earth-like surroundings, ensuring our every comfort. Look at that beautiful setting. This is what we call Lake Eden. These beautiful surroundings assist us mentally in advancing the Higher Power's vision for the benefit of all."

A good, warm, and wholesome discussion spontaneously occurs and, in the end, his father says, "You know, Son, my untimely and early departure from your world has been hard on everyone, and I wish I could have turned back the hands of time, but I couldn't. When your time is up in one world, accept it— plain and simple. It's up. Move on to your next assignment. I didn't realize that during my lifetime on earth. Then again, there were a lot of things that never crossed my mind about life, including, for that matter, the possibility of an afterlife. The higher power had bigger and better things for me to accomplish, and I was assured that my earth family, while set back by my early departure, would, in the end, survive well. The higher power treats us all well, and no greater expectations are placed on us, except to be respectful of others, be on guard, help our earthly family cruise through crises, and take on important assignments from time to time for the good of all. While I won't take any specific credit, I am always with you and all my remaining earth family clan, dropping hints and clues along the way. It is up to you to take what feels right and useful in winding yourself through the mysterious maze of life. So far, Son, you seem to have done all right for yourself and for others around you.

"You are, however— and I am truly sorry to surprise you—about to embark on a very special time in your life on earth, and that goes for you, too, Maggie. While I cannot go into any detail about your mission in life, you will sense what is right and what is not, I am sure. By the way, I guess you have already started out on your journey. Good luck, and may it be for the good of all. Open your creative minds to accept, not to question the possibilities, and open your logical minds to expand and absorb the 'what is/isn't' and the 'what isn't/is', and you will succeed for the good of all.

"I regret that I must cut this wonderful reunion off now, as I have other important work to do for the higher power. You know that I am always with you, and you are welcome to come back for short visits, as you can see I am only one small portal away."

Jake's father smiles, turns, and simply walks out of sight, leaving them to wonder. Jake and Maggie, holding each other closely, slip back through the portal and into the confines of their bedroom. Jake's head is spinning from the encounter, as he still is somewhat in a state of disbelief from the events that he has just born witness to.

Maggie says, "Jake, just believe. Do not question. This is all for a reason that will become clear someday."

CHAPTER 5
Reality Check

"Major Hall," Captain Gibson of Technical says, "Alpha 16 has observed Alpha 13, and all systems are operating as normal, sir. All external indicators suggest expected operations. Antennas are in constant movement during orbital shifts around earth, and lights for visual inspections are all functioning. We are just beginning the communication probe now, and we should have the first feed in a minute or so...

"Sir, the first feed has just been received. The expected functions are normal on Alpha 13. Alpha 16 has also shot a visual of Alpha 13. Screen functions and clarity are all normal."

"Well, if everything appears to be operating as expected, what is causing the black out? Do you have any ideas, Captain Gibson?"

"I think it will be wise to alter Alpha 16's orbit and position it between Alpha 14 and Alpha 15. This will permit Alpha 16 to operate within Iran. It will be a good test, and the results will confirm operations of the satellites, unless Alpha 16 blacks out. Then, we will have a real mystery on our hands."

"Okay, that sounds like a good plan, Captain, but in order to exercise that plan, we need authority from General Whitmore."

"I will see to that."

"Major, you have my okay to proceed with your intended plan," Colonel Britch states. "General Whitmore will have no difficulty with this decision. Trust me on this one. How much time are we talking to execute this maneuver Major," he asks. "What's the expected timing, Captain, to get all that needs to be done?"

"We will need to alter its computer databases to undertake the new orbit and observation. This can be done within one and a half hours, and it will take another fifteen minutes to slot into its new orbit. I'm not sure whether Iran will be in view at the time we slot it into its new orbit, so we may have to wait up to another twenty to forty minutes. I guess in about two hours time, sir."

Colonel Britch queries Major Hall, "How can this situation be? Does this mean that somehow Iran has developed some form of a shield or a wall preventing our view and our listening communication tracks from penetrating their air space?"

"Sir, it is too early to determine. It will take about a couple of hours for us to determine where to focus our attention."

"Keep working on it from your end and I will call the president."

"While the president is anxious to commence a meeting, we need to wait for Captain Gibson's prognoses."

A beehive of activity is taking place at the Eagle's Nest in a vane attempt to bring a resolution to the issue of Alpha 13, 14, and 15. Alpha 16 is carefully being slotted in between Alpha 14 and 15. In a very few minutes, Alpha 16 will be over Iran's air space. As the satellite nears Iran's air space, the tension builds, and the Eagle's Nest becomes unearthly quiet. Wavy lines and pure white static start to rattle across Alpha 16's monitor and then... a complete black out.

"Major Hall," Captain Gibson yells, "as suspected, sir, Alpha 16 blacked out as it approached Iran's air space. At least the Satellites are okay; that much we know. We just have a major mystery to solve in identifying and removing the interference."

"Colonel Britch, Major Hall here, sir. Alpha 16 blacked out over Iran's air space. We are sure the satellites are okay; however, we conclude there is some form of interference over Iran's air space."

"Okay, Major, I will advise General Whitmore. I think we have enough information to proceed with the presidential meeting."

The Joint Chiefs of Staff, Homeland Security, the NSA, the Eagle's Nest Director, and the FBI are called into an emergency meeting with the president in the Presidential Meeting Room at the White House.

"Okay, gentleman," the president says, "you now have been briefed by General Whitmore. I now have some good news, but unfortunately, there is also bad news, which is most haunting. Alpha 13 is functioning as was expected, and we are assuming that position also for Alpha 14 and 15. Gentlemen, what's haunting is that it's apparent that Iran has somehow developed a complete communications block. We don't know if it is some Electro-magnetic force field or what at this point. I don't have to remind anyone the gravity of this situation, considering Iran's president— that idiot— conjured up a serious alignment with North Korea's president. North Korea's General Lao and his atomic research scientists arrived last night in Iran, and we suspect there will be some joint developments undertaken on their atomic bomb project. He threatens to blow Israel off the map, and he is badgering us over our war efforts in Iraq and Afghanistan. North Korea's president has been flexing its muscles lately and has been riding the thin edge of the wedge, pushing his agenda, seeing how far he can go without creating an irreversible international incident. How coincidental that we have a communications black out now. Spread out getting every able body operative around the world working on a resolution and find out now what the hell is going on. This is critical. We cannot have this situation appear any other way than under control if we are forced to deal with other world leaders, the press, and most assuredly the opposition. We are under Red Alert. All forces on standby. Gentlemen, we meet at 06:00 sharp tomorrow."

CHAPTER 6
Is/Isn't

"It amazes me, Maggie. Here I am, almost a senior, but yet I feel that I am only in my infancy when it comes to grasping what life is all about. I really thought life was just about being a good wholesome person, being the best we can be with our knowledge and education and bringing others into this world to continue the life cycle. I might add, I think life is also about enjoying oneself along the way, together with family and friends, and cultivating good, solid relationships in every transaction in life. After meeting Dad, I guess I am confused about what life is all about. Where did we really come from, and is there an afterlife, not to mention the what is/isn't and the what isn't/is?"

"Yes," Maggie says, "life isn't as lucid as it seems."

"I understand that not all things are what they appear to be, Maggie. I haven't really studied this topic to grasp its full meaning. Possibly, it can be whatever the twisted and contorted mind encapsulates it to be. Maybe that's what Dad was getting at when he made the statement about is/isn't, etc. Maggie, just look how humans have evolved since the beginning of time. Who says we are fully evolved yet?"

"How, Jake?"

"Humans are far from perfect. We know that just by observing the simple errors of our way. Greed and lust seem to overcome such a vast number of humans from all races. Even today, our core brain still says kill if we're treed or, oh yes, for the love of a woman. Men just can't get women off the brain— no pun intended. But for me, it's only you, Babe."

"It better be," Maggie retorts in rapid fire, ushering curling acrid smoke beyond her luscious, sumptuous, rosy red lips. "Or you're toast. On second thought, I'll just bust your balls. I am just kidding, Darling. You scare me, Jake."

"Maggie, I'm having budding thoughts; we are truly limited by the lack of our own creativity. I know it sounds like I am speaking from the obvious, but Dad's visit puts hidden meaning to it. Wow! I now need to focus on that and seek clarity. I need to focus and train my brain to maximize my abilities. Jesus, life is so complex in so many ways. I just need to think. These past fifteen hours have been quite a mind-boggling escapade bordering on the now and vivid and then, the when and pellucid. You know, I think this is only the penult. No, I know it is just the beginning of what could be a long and convoluted journey to who knows where."

"I know it, too, Jake. This is/isn't thought needs to be dwelt on, and I'm with you, Baby. I'm also going to focus my thoughts on this."

"Hey, Sweetie, Katey is really giving me the evil eye ball this morning. Katey is in dire need of her walk so I will take her out now. You know how important it is for her to experience her daily dose of scents."

"Maggie, I guess, with all the changes to our lives recently, I have been ignoring her a bit, and she is laying a big guilt trip on me."

"Maggie, I'm really, really hungry this morning. I know its not Sunday, but can we have some of that oh so good country maple bacon, poached eggs, and toast?"

"You bet ya, lover. Anything for my baby. Anything your heart desires, because I love you so dearly."

"Thanks a bunch. I'll put on the coffee."

"Hey, Sweetie Pie, I can't believe it. I just completed a Level 3 Sudoku in forty-three seconds. There's no way could I do that yesterday or the day before! It would have taken at least ten minutes."

"Oh Maggie, and by the way, you won't believe

this: I just heard the coffee pot finish its brewing cycle...
Beep, beep, beep, beep, beep."

"Good for you, Jake."

"Coffee's ready. Maggie, it's been five years since I have heard that sound! Whatever is happening, but I like it."

"You know, Jake, after breakfast and Katey's walk, we should take your father's advice and really get to understand how the brain functions, and perhaps we can really facilitate our own growth and development. This could be a fun exercise, maybe scary, too, but there must be a good reason why all this strange stuff is happening to us."

"Count me in. I recall what Baden-Powell was purported to have said once many years ago: 'Be prepared.' Right now, I don't feel too prepared."

"Neither do I", Maggie commented.

"This has simply been a breakfast to die for, Darling! I'm going to take Katey for her walk of wonderful neighborhood scents. Ya wanna come?"

"Yes, I would love to, but not to the beach."

"No, no beach. Just a quick one around the block. I've had enough surprises this week myself."

"Me, too. I'll get a plastic bag and treats. I really feel like I need some fresh air, as my head is still in a fog or perhaps that vog."

CHAPTER 7
The Brain

"Jake, what really happened to us on the beach yesterday? I'm just feeling so different, so scared, and so confused, but I assure you that my love and feelings for you are still the same. Stronger I think."

"I don't know Maggie, but one thing has been gnawing at me.

"What's that, Jake?"

"I'm beginning to think something has triggered our brains, moving them on their evolutionary journey. Yet, how can it be so. We have been this way for centuries, I think. Our brains have somehow been activated in an odd way, and we are now starting to use more than that ten percent, which is the common myth among us unlearned ones."

"I haven't really noticed any difference, Jake, except for that little junket to see your father. What makes you think we are evolving?"

"You call slipping into a parallel universe little or no difference. When was it that you could achieve that before? That was an amazing feat not to mention it's already enriching our lives to boot. It's more than a feeling that I have, Maggie. There are little things happening to me, like my improved eyesight and hearing, not to mention my new found ability to do Sudoku. Something is definitely happening, Maggie."

"My only wish is that I could experience a major difference as you do."

"Okay, Maggie any ideas how we get started on this exercise, as my brain hasn't kick started yet."

"Jake, I recently read something on the brain and the purpose of its different components. I think this may be a good start. What do you think, Jake?"

"It works for me, I guess."

"Okay, Jake, I finally found the Internet article, and here is the diagram and explanation of the functioning brain. Okay, Jake, it's 9:00 A.M. Let's give it a go until lunch. Then, you can treat me to lunch at the Spot."

"Sounds like a good plan to me. I'm already hungry for one of the Triple-O Ooie Gooie Burgers and fries… A great start. This diagram looks like a lopsided tree."

"Let's get serious, Jake; we have much to learn in a short time span."

"Can't we just make love or something?"

"Oh! Get focused, Jake."

"Did you hear Katey groan? Look, she rolled her eyes in sheer disdain."

"Enough already; okay? Katey knows what the priority is right now, and besides, she really doesn't want to be disturbed… Jake, it appears the frontal lobe is primarily used for autonomic functions. For ease, let's call this the control panel. It regulates body function such as the heartbeat and body temperature, and it acts like a radiator or air-conditioning unit to control the temperature of the brain, etc."

"Frying the brain could blow the hard drive. Do you think, Maggie?"

"Speaking of hard drive, Jake, it seems that the midbrain, or temporal lobes, act in many ways like a hard drive. Of course, it serves many other functions, which we will look at later."

"Maggie, a sudden bright-light idea just came over me. Let's forget the brain for the moment. I'm not a scientist or medical expert. This discussion is simply not working for me. Anyway, we have already seen some subtle differences in our abilities; maybe other developments will naturally occur over time. Maybe we need to develop a new thinking concept so our development moves in more than one direction at a time. I do sense there is some urgency to our growth and development, but I have yet to define it."

"So, Jake, what do you have in mind?"

"Slipping through a portal or two into uncharted parallel universes is of high interest to me. That was an interesting experience for me this morning seeing my dad. I really want to thank you from the bottom of my warm heart for that awesome experience."

"You're welcome, Jake; it was fun and exciting for me, too."

"While I haven't achieved that feat yet, I think I understand how you did it, Maggie. I think that if we have the capability to slip through to Meadowbrook, we have the ability to slip into other parallel universes, that is, of course, if there are other universes to choose."

"Oh! There are other parallel universes, Jake. It's just that, at this moment, I am not sure what to expect if we were to just slip through one. Early this morning I sensed another portal while we were in Meadowbrook, but as I touched it with my hand, I received bad vibes. I just wasn't going to go there for fear, I guess, that that portal might put us in some form of peril. If we are going down that road we had better be highly intuitive."

"I agree, Maggie."

"Jake, why is it so important for you to explore other parallel universes?"

"I can't help but think that this may be an answer to rapid navigation and transportation. My sense tells me that our mission in life is not necessarily here, and we may need to travel throughout the world to find the answers we are looking for. We can't teleport ourselves as they apparently do on Star Trek, or at least I don't think we can. Levitation might help, but again, I haven't mastered that or even begun thinking seriously about it.

"I sense this new life we are about to embark on will require us to be fluid, so to speak. We must find a way to travel this universe at our own discretion and be discrete

30

about it. You can't just jump on a jet and travel the world looking for clues or ghosts. It takes too long to get wherever you want to go, and besides, we cannot afford it. Dad would have known that to!

"Dad said, 'You must open your creative brains to accept, not to question, the possibilities, and open your logical brains to expand and absorb the what is/isn't and the what isn't/is, and you will succeed for the good of all.' If that isn't a huge clue, then hit me over the head with a soft wake-up pill. Somehow we have to figure out how to use the parallel universes to do whatever it is we have to do?"

"You know, Jake, I think you are onto something, but venturing into uncharted areas may be too dangerous and ill-fated?"

"That's just the chance we will have to take."

"You know, I am not in the habit of taking on undue risk."

"I also need to trust your judgment and intuition, Maggie, when it comes to taking great leaps of faith. Just being a small step away from Meadowbrook suggests to me that we are only a small step away from anything or anywhere."

"That's a good possibility," Maggie said. "I hope you are right, but life never seems quite that easy. I'm sure there will be a few bumps along the way, perhaps even a few major potholes."

"I am not going into any unknown world without some level of protection, Maggie. I have packed a backpack filled with emergency supplies similar to what we would pack if we were about to experience an earthquake. Three days worth of water, dried foods, energy bars, medical kit, a small container to cook the dried foods, waterproof matches, two flashlights, enough spare batteries, and a candle in case there are romantic times in our journey. Oh yes, I forgot the blow-up pillow and the space blanket to keep us warm at night, just in case you are not up to the full charge in the wilds. Oh, I also packed a couple of toothbrushes and toothpaste. My 9-millimeter is strapped to my hip. I don't know if it would be useful if we encounter some wild beasts or civilizations not friendly to our invasion of their turf. I feel better just having it at my side; I know it works well in our world. Here is my Smith & Wesson 22-caliber semi-automatic pistol for you. Strap it on and pocket the extra clips. I have sufficient rounds of both 22-caliber and 9-millimeter in my pack to ward off a small army just in case we need them. By the way, if you expend a clip, don't throw it. You can reload them. No clip, no functional gun."

"Jake, I have only shot the gun once before, you are going to have to teach me how to operate this thing. If I have to use it, I would rather hit my intended target than shoot myself."

"Yep, no problem, I will give you a crash course before we go. Getting to understand what parallel universes are all about will obviously assist us. There is nothing better than comprehending the environment we are operating in. I see this as a great learning experience, Maggie, and I am sure this adventure will assist us in the future, whatever the future holds for us. Are you ready to go Maggie?"

"Yes, but I am not clear on what we want to achieve, and I need to know the game plan. Right now that is not clear to me."

"Good point. I have been so excited about this adventure that clarity has eluded me. Sorry, Babe. First, I would like to see how many parallel universes we can enter. The purpose of entering them is to determine if we can garner anything useful from them. For example: Where is it taking us? Can it deliver us somewhere in the world we might want or need to go? Is it a short cut? Is it friendly or hostile? If it is friendly, can we identify any resources to assist us in the future? I don't know what I am expected to do in the future, so I need to seek out as many potential resources from wherever I can derive them. I am also looking for overlapping universes, Maggie. If they exist, then they would be useful in listening into earthly conversations without detection. I guess we will be like the early explorers before us. As they traveled, they created maps so others could follow or so they could successfully return from their journeys. I want to understand if there is any connection. Can we weave in and out and travel our universe and successfully return? The safe return is the big one. Not having the pleasure of having been through this before leaves a lot of holes in establishing a game plan. I have outlined a general plan of sorts; however, it could go off the rails at any moment, and we must be fluid and go with the flow."

"Okay Jake, I guess I am as comfortable as I can be. I agree charting unknown waters is difficult to anticipate at best, and we must use our intuitiveness and be ready to alter course whenever. So I guess I am ready to embark this adventure. Jake, cuddle me, please. Just the thought of doing what we are about to do scares me to no end. What if we don't make it back here? What about Katey girl? What about my boys? What about your mom, children, grandchildren, and brothers? I love life as we have it. It just seems that we are taking such a risk, and for what?"

"I hear you, Babe. I, too, worry about those things, and life has been pretty easy to live with. It's fun and loving without worry, and we are working toward our life goals. I sense that there is a greater risk if we turn our backs to this. We are trying to prepare ourselves with information and arm ourselves with special talents… FOR THE GOOD OF ALL I believe we are moving in the necessary direction, or we would otherwise be given a hint or clue. I haven't seen any bread crumbs lying around, have you?"

"Spare me, Jake."

"So, Sweetie, are you ready to go?"

"No! Jake, you haven't shown me how to use this damn thing that's strapped to my hip."

"Oops! I forgot. I'm just too anxious to get started… Okay, Maggie, withdraw the gun from its holster, placing your trigger finger on the trigger guard and not on the trigger itself. You should always get into the habit of placing your trigger finger on the trigger guard, as it reduces the chances of accidental discharge. I want you to eject the ammunition magazine. There is a button to push on the handle in the forward portion of the handle or hand grip. Push it now, and it will release the magazine. The gun is still dangerous, as we now need to inspect the barrel for the round in the chamber. To do so, simply pull back the recoil located at the rear top of the gun. Good, no bullet was ejected, as I did not place a round in the chamber. The gun, even though inspected, should not be assumed to be safe. In other words, don't point it at anyone. Guns considered safe have killed. Accidents can happen. Are you Okay with what you have just done?"

"Yes, that is quite clear."

"Okay then, while the gun is unloaded, let's deal with the proper shooting stance and the aiming of the gun. While this gun has no recoil, it is still suggested that you stand with legs twelve to eighteen inches apart to ensure good balance. Release the safety mechanism, which is the red button near the top rear of the gun. Now the gun will fire if the trigger is squeezed. Then, raise the gun to an intended target, with your arm out straight and the gun held perpendicular to yourself. If the gun is listing, then the bullet will not fly where you think it should go; it will, either yaw left or gee right of the intended target. Does that feel comfortable?"

"Yes."

"As you are raising your arm to the intended target, your trigger finger should carefully be relocated and rested lightly on the trigger. Now slowly squeeze the trigger. You squeeze rather than pull the trigger. Pulling causes the gun to move off the intended target. Now reload the ammunition clip and cock the gun by pulling back on the recoil at the top back of the gun. This action just loaded a round into the hole or chamber and is ready to be fired. Now set the safety lock and holster your gun. If you need to use the weapon, all you do is remove it from the holster, release the safety lock, aim, and squeeze the trigger. If you need to fire another round just, squeeze the trigger again. You currently have nine rounds in the clip and one round in the chamber. Let's pray that we don't need to use these weapons. Are you ready to go now?"

"Yes, but please don't leave me anywhere, Jake. Stay with me."

"It's a done deal, Babe. I promise."

CHAPTER 8
A Curious Journey

"I must leave it to you, Darling. Take us to a new, friendly parallel universe."

"Hold my hand, Jake," Maggie says, and they slip into a strange place.

"Jesus," Jake says, "just where in hell are we. This place is so goddamned eerie, gray, boring, and dull."

"I'm not sure, Jake."

As Maggie and Jake begin their search through this murky existence, they become aware of the fact that it appears to be inhabited by millions and millions of empty human carcasses. As in Meadowbrook, no one seems to takes notice of their presence, and yet they can simply reach out and touch their bodies, not that they would want to touch them, given their appalling and, in some cases, mutilated condition.

Jake and Maggie watch in utter amazement the people or mere shells of people walking aimlessly with no agenda, no enthusiasm, expressing no real life, arms stretched downward by their sides, heads bowing down as if they were focusing on placing just one foot ahead of the next, step after step after step, just walking, walking, walking to nowhere and keeping to themselves, not acknowledging anyone, just maintaining the order in which they appear to be, in some reasonably fashioned organized line. For as far as the eye can observe, they keep coming and coming and coming.

There are young ones, middle aged ones, mothers with babies, mothers with none, some totally mutilated, some held together by the tattered remains of what appears to be an explosive vest, some old ones, some sick ones. Where they are going remains a mystery. While their destination is a mystery, one thing's for sure: It is a one way street. They all walk from east to west, from sunrise to murky sunset.

Battered bodies— one looks like he has been hit by a train; another has been beheaded; others have broken limbs, parts torn off their desperate bodies; and many look tormented from love-loss or other disappointments in their lives. People are all so pale, so lifeless in many ways, their blood all but drained, leaving only their cadavers to transport what is left. What a sad state in which to see these souls existing, without expression, without purpose, without a will. Lost souls they are. This is bloody morbid, but a good eye opener, they think.

Casting their eyes over the barren, desolate landscape, they observe a disturbing number of broken cadavers. It is apparent that they have just given up on their judgments, unable, unwilling to carry on. They just leave the pack and crumbled to pieces.

"Maggie," Jake whispers with excitement, "I recognize that fellow over there. He's John Woodward, a former executive for one of America's telephone companies. He was responsible for the deaths of seven people, as a result of crashing his car into a van carrying a large family on the I-5 just south of Seattle. He was more than a bit tipsy the night of the crash that also killed him some four years ago. The only survivor was a young, buxom blonde bombshell who walked away with minor scratches. Its' odd that she was with John that night, as he seemed to be a happily married man, married to a beautiful ex-cheerleader of the Seattle Seahawks, and they were raising three children. Such a waste," Jake states.

"It looks to me as if he was a philanderer, Jake?"

John acknowledges Jake's presence, thus turning his caved in head and his taped together right leg toward him, looking most distressed. Wanting to say something but unable to, he simply turns back again and just keeps on

37

walking, as if walking were the only thing he were able to do or wanted to do or were ordered to do. The entire population is doing the exact same thing: walking, walking, and walking some more.

This confirms to them that they are not capable of thought; they are mere shells of their former selves, waiting for their judgment. It makes Jake and Maggie want to be only good in life so as not to be destined to this misery. What possibly can their stories be that they have been thrust into this existence? There cannot be any peace for their souls. Poor souls!

If they have been waiting this length of time for their judgment, then the potential for metempsychosis to occur is likely beyond comprehension. Perhaps this is a good thing. One may recognize old souls in some people. Perhaps these people have always been good and decent human beings. These souls in waiting, however, need not be a part of life or create new life.

"Jake, this place reminds me of Purgatory, the holding place for those who haven't clearly demonstrated their essentials for entry into an everlasting peaceful existence in a place like Meadowbrook. They are awaiting the Higher Power's Judgment about their life on Earth."

"Scary thought; don't you think, Maggie?"

"I never would have thought that so many people fall into this category, Jake. Most people seem to be good in exercising life skills, abiding by rightful morals and values, and generally being all-round good humans. At least, that is my impression of those we associate with."

"This doesn't surprise me a bit, Maggie. Twenty or maybe thirty years ago, yes, it would have surprised me, but with what I see happening today— street violence among our youth, the myriad of gang development, growth and activity in credit card scams, identity theft, the drug trade, prostitution trade and the violence associated with it— far too many of the members of our urban societies are down and out, high on drugs one minute and crazy car grabbers the next. Residential and commercial crime is running amok. A growing number of commuters are becoming bullies and are demonstrating road rage, creating hell on our highways. Politicians are involved in self-rewarding scandals, and the liberal views of the general population base all contribute to a questionable view of behavior on Earth. Corporate executives of big or small organizations are screwing their shareholders for self-gain, and government bureaucracy is ever bloating at the seams in self-importance and self-indulgence. It's like we are re-entering the Sodom and Gomorra stage of existence. God forbid. We had better get a collective grip on this rampant destruction of our society and business world to ward off economical and societal chaos. I expect this place to be jam-packed in the next ten years. Yep, this place will be so jammed-packed and the lineups for judgment so long, it will make our health care system look good."

Now that Jake's rant on society is over, Maggie, from a somewhat cynical perspective, expresses her general agreement, with a sigh. "Come on, Sweetie, I don't think we are going to learn much from the experience in this rotting hole, except that it is apparent that we must continue to live honorable lives and maintain a clear focus on wants and desires for ourselves and family balanced with and for the good of all; let's find another portal.

"Jake, one thing that I have learned is that our world seems to be going to Hell in a hand basket. This is a testament of a world far more troubled than I had ever imagined. This should not be; whatever happened to morals and values and the general human behavior for the good of all. What I have witnessed here today appears to be the direct result of nothing less than sheer greed and selfishness."

"Maggie, the Western World appears to be a desperate society spiraling down the self-destructive path of liberalism. Oh my God, should I live to be a hundred, please never let the liberal-minded run this country again, as we may never be able to save it if we do. The Eastern World! Well that's another story. They appear to be on the brink of their own demise, given such radical views being expressed: their hatred for western ways and their oppression of women. Of course, we can't forget the suicide bombers who blow themselves and other innocent people up, all in the belief that twenty-some-odd virgins will await them in the afterlife. Some people just don't get it. It's the oldest con game in the world, and what would you do with twenty-odd women anyway. One is surely enough. Well, it is for me."

"Okay, hold my hand, Jake, this is a warm one and…Oh Jesus, no…"

CHAPTER 9
Early Morning

"Gentlemen," the president states impatiently, "cut the bullshit. Brief me on the facts."

A long pause. "Well I'll be dammed, ya'll dam well skunked or what?"

"General Whitmore, sir. The truth of the matter is that we are no further ahead in solving this issue now than we were yesterday afternoon. Every deployed resource has reported back with a similar response: unable to detect a communications wall or block. Communications within the country are all running normally. Television and radio all appear to be functioning as normal. The only interesting feedback we have received is that from outside the country of Iran. Internet from Iran is believed to only work one way, and that would be out. The NSA reports its surveillance of Internet correspondence coming out of Iran as normal. Not more than an hour ago, the President of Iran stood at his pulpit, as he usually does, and beaked off to his people about common everyday nonsense. No one seems to be acting any differently now than they did the day before, and our Iranian operatives are not being hassled by the authorities any more than they were in the past. That missive came from an operative that just left Iran and reported in. Things are pretty much as they were before. It's truly puzzling, Mr. President."

"Puzzling," the president retorts, "Given all the goddamn intelligence and resources at our disposal, I can't believe we are coming up dry. What are we missing? What the hell are we missing, damn it?

"General Whitmore," the president states, "you will put together a team of twenty of our best-trained covert operatives to infiltrate the most secluded and secretive atomic research sites and military installations in Iran. You and your team of experts will uncover the shroud of secret operations Iran is so sinisterly involved in. We are going into Iran, and you have seven days to get prepared. We have a desperate need to get to the root of this issue and remove this damn communications block. Our people are at extreme risk, and now we must risk the lives of twenty more for the good of all. Yes, each and every one of us existing on this earth is in peril. Every day we are unable to conduct surveillance on the goings-on in Iran is another day closer to the potential ill-fate of the Western World. It's intolerable that we, the United States of America, have been hoodwinked, and its specifically horrifying that impending peril has been set upon our people. Any questions gentlemen?"

"Mr. President, sir, General Whitmore. We intend to carry out your orders, but seven days isn't sufficient or optimal to recruit, prepare our team, and strategically build our tactical mission. With all due respect, sir, fourteen days would be pushing it at best, given we only have one opportunity to succeed."

"General Whitmore, we have over 1,120,000 men and women watching out for the security of this nation. With those resources available, you will be given priority service to optimize the success of twenty of our best to directly infiltrate Iran. I believe you underestimate our capabilities. Are you up to the task or what?"

"Yes, Sir."

"Who do you have in mind to lead the covert infiltration, General?"

"Sir, Colonel Zorrograpidis, a seasoned covert operative of the U.S. Navy Seals. I consider him the best soldier we have, and the most brilliant mind."

"Uh huh! I will be back to you, General. I need to be updated on a daily basis about the critical steps in the progress toward our mission. Are there any theories from the bright lights in the think tank at the Pentagon? I've got the New Democratic Majority House Leader literally climbing my butt, demanding that I bring her up to date. She senses, given the shroud of secrecy and a scurry of activity going on, that a national security issue is arising. If she only knew, it would blow her fucking mind. We can't afford to allow anyone to know that we are currently buffaloed, damn it. The media smells a scoop and has literally camped themselves here at the White House. All they know at this moment is that their communications have ceased going to their reporters, journalists, and other media people in Iran, and they are demanding answers."

"I need to spin some convincing story line to thwart the goddamn over-reactionary, meddling press, and I need to do it now. General Whitmore, get your boys working on some plausible theory."

"Yes, sir, and furthermore, Mr. President, the Pentagon is currently running probability assessment scenarios and will report their theoretical outcomes and assumptions A.S.A.P."

"Yes, that's good, but 'probable' and 'theoretical' don't quite cut it, General; we need certainty."

CHAPTER 10
Curious Journey: A Living Hell

Both Jake and Maggie scream as they hurl into the center of this new universe, rolling, tumbling end-over-end, in what seems to be an endless free fall. The sudden change in the ambient temperature is all too puzzling and brings them into an instant and complete body sweat. Where they are going they do not know, but they wonder if they can survive. It is, nonetheless, becoming difficult to breathe. With complete abruptness, they suddenly fall to a halt into a bed of warm, wretched-smelling ashes.

"Jesus, where are we," Maggie?"

"Thank God for soft landings!" says Maggie. "Jake, I don't think it's a good idea to use the name Jesus in here. Judging from what little I see, this has to be Hell."

"Maggie, I agree, and maybe the use of the word 'God' isn't such a great idea either."

"Welcome to this living HELL, a hell of an existence that you could never imagine exists, but you mere humans don't know your real environment," booms one husky voice.

"Ha! Ha! Ha! The only universe where there are no rules, petty laws, regulations, or by-laws, no goody-goody-two-shoes or shit-filled Twinkies here either," a devilish, sinister voice booms out. It's every man, woman or child for him/herself. Be self-indulgent, lecherous, murderous, and crude or end up tied to a burning stake, left only to suffer the cruelest of pain, hurt, and merciless self-destruction."

"This place is nothing but a crazy farm! People or mere image-remains of people are simply brutalizing each other. It's gross!" Jake gasps. "Watch out, Maggie. Keep an eye on that guy behind the mutilated marble alter. He has a huge butcher knife, and it looks like he is well-experienced in using it."

"I am having difficulty concentrating on any one occurrence, Jake. There is just so much gore and bloodletting going on around us."

"Thank God people, or hulks of people past, have ignored us so far."

Crack.

"Ugh, oh shit, Maggie, I just crushed someone's skull! Jesus, this place is like an unorganized, old auto junk yard, body parts scattered and strewn everywhere. What a goddamn pig sty this place is."

"I really can't comphrehend this place Jake, there is nowhere on earth that people or mere shells of people past behave like this!"

I don't either Maggie, this is all beyond me, nothing that I have learned during my journey in life represents what is going on here, It's a mystery.

"Jake, I hope you don't recognize anyone here. I don't know if I can cope with the outcome. I need to get back to Katey and the kids and the sanity of our once wonderful life... Oh shit, Jake. Oh! Oh! SHIT! I recognize that girl standing by the burning Cathedral. That's Cherry Lobbit! She worked in South Carolina, coaching us in building our transition team. While I was there, she beheaded her husband as he was sleeping and then cut off his penis. She apparently then jammed his penis into his mouth and shoved his head between his legs. She claimed that her husband was sleeping with another man."

Cherry recognizes Maggie and instantly begins screaming at the top of her fiery lungs in an unrecognizable gibberish, pulling a small cutlass from her side. Running toward Maggie, wielding this fancy, even cutesy cutlass, frothing at the mouth, seething through her nostrils, her blackened eyes are likened to deadly daggers dripping with curdling blood, ready to strike a deathly blow.

A gunshot roars off from Jake's 9-millimeter, hitting Cherry in her left breast. The bullet explodes through her backside, spreading dried and rancid chards of dead flesh in every direction. Maggie stands there shaking in utter disbelief, with her mouth agape, then slowly turns toward Jake and screams in terror. Maggie's screaming awakens these demons to their presence. A number of Satan's Finest immediately take advantage of the girl's plight, reducing her to mere bubbles as they watched in horror. They slip away to a safer spot to regain their bearings while some of Satin's Finest feast on the girl's rotting remains.

"Jesus, Jake— now you got me saying it— we have gone from bad to worse! We've got to find a way out of this universe and fast."

Satin's Finest, having now consumed every morsel of Cherry Lobbit, begin focusing their attention on Maggie and Jake. Milling about, chanting some unintelligible sounds, they swiftly raise their small arms and began charging toward them with renewed bloodthirsty lust on their minds.

Maggie and Jake begin running and running as fast as they can, with Jake holding Maggie's hand in a vain attempt to motivate her short legs to move faster. The gap between Satin's Finest and them is closing... and closing fast. Maggie reaches— in reality, stretches— for a portal and drags Jake and herself through it just as Jake feels the air whoosh behind his head from a swinging cutlass.

CHAPTER 11
Curious Journey: Incredible Discovery

Tripping upon entry into yet another parallel universe, they roll together down a sizeable hill and end up in a field of tall, green grass, like an oasis in a desert.

"I don't have any idea, where we are, Jake? I didn't have time to get my bearings. It seems quite serene— a bit of a hot but pleasurable climate. Perhaps this parallel universe is friendly?"

Jake and Maggie appear to have landed in a vast, flat, desert-like area. Save for a small, green, lush oasis, it is very arid, with only a few cacti growing and a bit of dead tumbleweed gently blowing across it by way of the warm southern winds.

In the distance and far to the West of their particular landing site, the faint sound of what seams like running water can be heard. They quickly decide it is their best bet to seek out the water source. They walk for what seems to be an endless period of time. All the while, the sound of water flowing becomes stronger and stronger.

The overland terrain is quite easy to negotiate, and every once in a while they see a scorpion dash off as if it doesn't want to tangle with humans. One rattler is spotted sunning itself on the small but orderly arranged outcropping of stone. Neither the snake nor Maggie and Jake sensing a threat toward each other, they pass at a safe distance. The sun is high in the sky, and the temperature is now reaching one hundred ten degrees. Thankfully, they have brought water with them; it brings relief from the brutal sun's rays. They finally come upon a simply magnificent waterfall cascading approximately one thousand five hundred feet down to the bottom of a wide and lush canyon below.

"Come on, Maggie, let's head down to the canyon floor and explore."

"You have got to be kidding, Jake. I'm no mountain climber."

"We can take our time and choose our descent carefully. We are meant to be in this universe and there is nothing up here, so we must, at least, based on a calculated risk, venture down and find whatever we are meant to find."

Searching for the right spot to start their descent is a difficult task, as neither of them have any prior experience. They come upon what looks like the remains of an old trail and decide that it is likely their best bet. Either animals or humans have used this trail in the distant past, so while it looks menacing, it is likely somewhat negotiable.

It is a tough journey traversing over large rocks, sliding down some short but scary chutes, skinning their hands and scrapping their butts, hoping not to over-shoot their intended target. Fortunately, the amount of loose debris is minimal, and the trail soon started to smooth out, at last making the rest of the journey quite pleasurable.

During their decent Maggie and Jake observe a plesent temperature adjustment and the existence of relatively high humity. They also took the time to notice their changed surrounding and the sun's position in the sky. Maggie, the sun is in the northern sky, so we must now be in the southern hemishire. At home, the sun rises in the eastern sky and moves south until it sets in the western horizon. I would suggest given the sun's position we are somewhere between the Equator and the Tropic of Capricorn.

In the distance, they can hear birds singing, and the buzzing of some bees and other insects comes into their hearing range. If there are birds, there will be animals, and then, perhaps there is a good chance human life may exist, they think. With the prospect of meeting another civilization fresh in their minds, they advance with greater vigor and perhaps with a little less caution. They are awed by what they see and liken it to the rain forest that they live in.

Walking the canyon floor proves most interesting, and soon they come across something that is interesting yet quite baffling: Cut lines in the rock floor appear. They are perfectly straight lines running from south-southwest to north-northeast. The lines are about one hundred feet apart. There are also intersecting lines running south-southeast to north-northwest, and these lines are spaced one hundred fifty feet apart. It appears to be some form of a grid or perhaps an ancient navigational aid. These appear to be ancient lines, likely carved thousands of years ago.

Maggie and Jake continue to walk the grid lines until they cease, and they come to where a very large circle is carved into the flat rock floor. The circle's circumference is about one thousand feet. Circle lines appear every ten feet until the final circle is ten feet in circumference. This is the bull's eye of a very large circle.

"Do you think this was a landing site for a U.F.O., Jake?"

"Good for you, Maggie. I do believe you are right."

"I remember reading something about an unexplained navigational aid similar to what we are standing on. It is located somewhere in South America, I believe, and it may well have been tied into the Inca or pre-Inca civilization. I could be wrong; it was so many years ago. I have a wonderful memory; it's just short."

While they are riveted and captivated by this ancient wonder, they soon find themselves encircled by a life form totally foreign to them. While there appears to be no imminent sense of threat, these aliens, by looks, disgust them. These strange-looking creatures are eyeing them very closely, muttering to each other in a truly foreign chatter.

After what seems to be an eternity, a very tall and thin creature steps forward with apparent authority over the others. Jake and Maggie suddenly sense a creepy, eerie feeling in their guts, thinking they are about to meet their waterloos.

It's difficult to accurately reflect the image standing about five feet in front of them actually, because their fear level is rising. They clearly are not prepared to encounter what is standing before them. They can't turn and run or otherwise escape either. Part of their difficulty exists because they cannot distinguish gender, if gender differences exist for these creatures.

"It" is about eight feet tall with long thin legs equipped with knees and feet that have six toes joined by a web like skin, a slender long body, four arms of similar length, with each hand sporting six long fingers joined by what appears to be a duck web. Its skin is bumpy and the skin color is mottled, pale white to tan. Its head is most peculiar, long and thin, devoid of hair, with pointed long ears like Spock's on Star Trek, a flat nose, three eyes— one located in the center of the forehead— and a mouth shaped similar to that of a Coho salmon.

The alien creature slowly turns around to signal to the other creepy similar looking aliens that there is nothing to fear. Jake and Maggie observe a single eye just above the nape of the creature's neck. There is no visible chin; the head just slopes-off and joins a thin neck. There are no visible genitals or other distinguishing features, so it is impossible to determine gender. Perhaps if they had more time and were less apprehensive about their own well-being, a difference could well be found.

Standing face-to-face, the creature mutters some foreign gibberish. Jake responds in English stating, "I am unable to understand your language."

It— and "It" is only referred to as "It" due to the lack of gender identification— immediately switches its language to English and says, "Welcome to Naranna, our land away from our homeland Annaran."

They just stand there stunned at their discovery; their jaws drop, and then hesitantly and nervously, they introduce themselves stating, "We... uh... we uh... are from North America on the planet Earth."

It laughs and exclaims, "We share the same earth but live in a neighboring parallel universe."

Its laugh lightens them up a bit, thinking they can't be all that bad— ugly, yes, but not necessarily bad.

"I am Koidon, the leader of my people. We are of the Exzistan Civilization, the oldest and most advanced civilization from the planet Annaran. We occupy the continent Exzista, which is similar to South America on Earth. Our planet is located just beyond Earth's solar system, and it is very similar in climate, landscape, rivers, and oceans, but it is about half again the size of Earth. We left our home planet of Annaran many years ago, as life's existence was becoming difficult, actually life-threatening. Annaran, was once a vibrant, lively planet with lush vegetation, ample water, and food sources. Annaran had a nice warm climate year round, very stable weather conditions, and a thriving economy that provided a luxurious lifestyle for all.

"A very large meteorite hit the planet and knocked it off its axis. That's when our difficulties on Annaran began. The skies grew angry; many ferocious storms were endured; our water seemed to disappear deep beneath the soil; and the food sources began to dry up. We had the capability as a developed civilization to move to another planet; reluctantly and without real choice, we relocated to Earth.

"Earth is a wonderful planet; however, we are so different from human beings that we simply had to move to a parallel universe and share the beauty of the land with others while living a wonderful, prosperous existence undiscovered. We, as a civilization, have developed our brains to such an extent that we can change ourselves to look, act, speak and behave like other life forms. This has ensured our security since leaving Annaran. Through our travels, we have encountered many hostile civilizations and wild beasts. Unfortunately, some of these civilizations have found their way to Earth.

"Our infiltration into your society occurred about fifty years ago. We came not as hostile aliens but to gain knowledge and to get to know and understand your civilization, thinking that someday we may be able to co-exist. How did we infiltrate your society undetected? We simply changed our form to conform to human specifications. We now know, through our experiences, that co-existence is not possible today, as humans have not developed sufficiently to accept unlike civilizations such as Exiztans. Earthlings are still dealing with inter-racial difficulties, personal and business greed, and the wrath of various religious zealots wanting to convert others to unwanted beliefs, values, and morals, leading us to know that much insecurity, immaturity, and jealously continues to exist, blocking our ability to co-exist. Your civilization is where our civilization was three hundred years ago.

"That's our saga in abbreviated form. There is still much more we could tell, perhaps at a different time."

Maggie and Jake stand spellbound at what they have just heard. Not wanting to interrupt for fear that the Exiztans with have mood swings or that they will leave the impression they are not interested in their story, Jake and Maggie remained silent. After all, they feel that they are now on their turf.

Koidon chortles with an affectionate smile. "You two seem to have broken through a mind barrier. Seemingly, you have begun developing your brains to accept the what is/isn't. That is a major evolutionary jump for humankind, and you are on that cusp of change. We are shocked and surprised to see you two, as we didn't anticipated humans were even close to realizing the next evolutionary change. We did not want to miss the chance of this interception, and we hope we have not scared you to excess."

Jake and Maggie still just stand there, stunned and speechless.

"I will now change my appearance to reflect that of yours to demonstrate our intelligence, and I will surely become more pleasant to your eyes," Koidon says, giving Maggie a wink.

As if metamorphosis were occurring or a snake were shedding its skin, Koidon's appearance suddenly changes to that of an earthlike human.

"Wow, how did you do that, Koidon?"

"It is simply mind over matter, nothing more or nothing less. You must realize that your brain is more powerful than any computer will ever be, as it is also stimulated by deep powerful emotional responses. The brain, as we have just observed, is more multi-dimensional than ever believed and has a capacity to connect the mind and body in ways never before imagined. One day, you will likely develop the advanced skill to turn yourself into whatever life form you want or need for your own protection; you just need time and patience to evolve your brain's capacity. It is important that you develop one step at a time and fully understand the magnitude of that growth."

"Do you really think that is possible for us Earth people to accomplish such a feat?"

"Yes, you are on your way to discovering many useful skills and abilities, and remember, focus on what is/isn't and what isn't/is."

Maggie and Jake look at each other as if they have seen a ghost, both thinking how unbelievable and perhaps coincidental it is that Koidon would use those terms: "what is/isn't" and "what isn't/is". That reference has been directed toward them a number of times over the past couple of days from different sources. How uncanny!

Again, words to ponder carefully, they think.

"Come with me and view firsthand a portion of our humble community. You will not see the automobile such as you have in your civilization."

"How do you get around, particularly to places of considerable distance?"

"Ah, we simply teleport ourselves to where ever we wish to go. If it is only a short distance, we use levitation to facilitate our ground coverage. Levitation is also a wonderful way to travel if viewing the environment is on your mind.

"While we have industry to serve our requirements, we have developed ecosystems to ensure there is no pollution created. The industry's ecologically damaging output is simply converted into energy that supplies electricity for our use. We have lived through the scourge of pollution created by our civilization on Annaran, and we simply have learned not to pollute but respect this land.

"Again, we do not have housing such as you have; however, we are most comfortable with what we have created. Money is not an issue. There is no greed here. We all live a life of luxury, and all of us possess genuine purpose in life to better ourselves academically, mentally, and physically. We value family interests, self-interests, self-worth, and expression and seek to offer to others our discoveries. This is fundamental to the continued evolution of our civilization, as is peace. Here is where we dwell. We have carved out our shelter from these mountain cliffs. These cliffs face the North, giving us maximum exposure to the sun. The radiant heat warms the stones, which, in turn, emit heat during the evening hours. Our climate is so moderate that being cold is never an issue. You likely didn't notice that electrical wiring does not exist and, therefore, we have avoided the unsightliness of sky pollution. We have developed a wireless electrical transmission system that supplies our entire universe. Electricity is broadcast like radio waves, and our individual collector boxes absorb sufficient power to supply our needs. We discovered, by accident, that by intertwining the long and short wave radio signals, protecting the integrity of the waves with plasma, permitted the transmission of electrical power for thousands of miles with a minimal of loss. Coating the waves with plasma protects or shields our people from the potential harmful effects of electrical transmission. There are no electrical outlets, as our electrical equipment likewise draws its required power wirelessly from our collector boxes.

"Ah, this is Foinama, my revol, the love of my life. In your world, she is considered my wife."

"Welcome to our home," Foinama says warmly, as she motions them inside. Foinama saw them nearing, and prior to their arrival, she changed herself into a human form.

"This is Jake and Maggie from North America."

"It's very nice to meet you."

"Wow, your cliff home is wonderful, cheerful, warm, and much larger than I would have anticipated," Maggie says. "I shouldn't be surprised, but I see that your needs for sustaining everyday life are somewhat similar to our needs."

Koidon states his pleasure in seeing their growing evolution and suggests that this development, and what is likely to be experienced in the near future, will be very beneficial to humankind and all other living existences.

"I must admit that I have become worried, particularly in the past few years, that earth is in serious jeopardy due to the global unrest and the threat of nuclear contamination. The U.S.A., Great Britain, and Canada are on the right track; however, diplomacy needs to be bolstered, and warfare needs to decline. We experienced similar conditions in Annaran with the clashing of the various civilizations. Much violence occurred, and heavy pollution created by those clashes actually doomed some civilizations in the extreme North and South Polar Regions of our planet. Then the meteorite that shifted Annaran off its axis eventually made life unbearable for all remaining civilizations, as I mentioned to you earlier."

"Koidon," Jake says, "how did you ever find a place that looks and feels so welcoming and homey and has a pleasant climate? Your location choice to build your cliff shelters also provides you with an exquisite view of Naranna. It is such a beautiful-looking place; we would consider this paradise back home."

"We were drawn to this area of the world based on our previous life experiences in Annaran. While many differences exist between the two planets, there are just as many similarities. The make-up of a planet that is inhabitable by life forms does not occur by accident, but rather by design. The Maker must ensure a balance occurs, ensuring our every need. We simply followed our senses and discovered this lush, friendly environment."

"I cannot believe the incredible beauty that abounds: crystal clear, deep blue lakes and beaches lined with swaying and the most awesome-looking palm trees. The array of beautiful flowers and shrubbery that adorn the walkways, grassy areas, and fields adds wholesomeness to this peaceful, tranquil living that I know you must enjoy. What is evidently amazing is that there is no smog in the air or soot or other harmful fallout to be observed."

"We do enjoy our surroundings immensely, and we will do everything in our power to ensure its ever-lasting tranquility and beauty. Fishing is one of our greatest past times, as the solitude serves a dual purpose. One: We use the time waiting for a fish to strike our lines to expand our knowledge by testing new information or new-found knowledge against our brains power. Secondly, catching a fish is a thrill, and to have the skill to land the fish without hurting it is even more enjoyable and challenging for sure. Of course, we usually return the fish to the lake, as we use barbless hooks here, and we believe a catch and release program is vital to sustaining a valuable pastime."

"Koidon," Jake says, "we have been away longer than we have intended, and our Katey— that is our pet dog— is home alone and likely would appreciate a little outdoor time!"

"Katey would love Naranna; you know a dog's outdoor pleasure is mostly about scents. Bring Katey on your next visit; we would love to meet her. Naranna is filled with wonderful fragrances. Foinama and I would appreciate your return, as it is enjoyable conversing with you, but we also have much more to share with you."

"We would love to return, and we will bring Katey. Come on, Maggie, while I would love to stay here longer, we must continue our quest to understand our mission and develop our skills for the good of all."

"Seek and ye shall find," Koidon states. "For you, the journey's end is not as far off as you think. You have made significant progress."

Jake and Maggie slip out of the Naranna portal and, with their newly acquired navigational sense, arrive home without incident. Katey is very happy to see them, as usual, and needs a jaunt in the grass.

"Well, Sweetie," Jake says, "we only meant this to take us to lunch time, but here it is 5:00 P.M., and am I ever hungry. How about we dine at the White Spot tonight? I can taste the burger and fries now, and a glass of white wine or two will go down ever so smoothly."

"You're on, Jake, and I guess that I am buying... with pleasure."

"Thanks for getting us home safely, Jake."

"Thanks, but don't thank me. It was you that did the navigation, Maggie."

"Thank you, Darling."

Over dinner Maggie and Jake reflect back on what they have experienced during their day. Maggie is just amazed that there are other civilizations sharing the planet, and while they unto themselves have similar needs, they are so grossly different in their make-up.

"I guess it reflects the environment and world they came from."

"I, too, am agog over what we witnessed," Jake states.

"I understand the purpose of Purgatory and Hell parallel universes, given that we truly are in need to rid ourselves of— I don't know; I'm looking for better words; they're not coming— ah... looking for a place to dump our human waste, so to speak."

"Naranna is a delightful environment that I would like to know better."

"Me, too," Maggie says. "They seem to be a well-principled civilization, having extreme intelligence and also wanting to continue their collective evolution."

"I really like Koidon," Jakes states. "No matter what his appearance is, I know that we can learn a lot from him."

Maggie agrees and further states, "The persona of these people is warming and especially comfortable. It is a joy to be with such positive, forward reaching people. Foinama is a very special individual whom, I believe, I can become quite close to. Did you notice the neatness and high level of organization that exists in their household? It blew me away; where does she get the time?"

"They have three hundred years on us. Wow, let us hope and pray it doesn't take our civilization that long to get to where they are. Maybe we can be an influence in that regard, but as usual, in our society, we have too many negative thinkers who are ever so resistant to change that they impede progress."

"Oh, don't be so pessimistic, Jake. Maybe the naysayers will respond to change if they can see it's not political— not for the betterment of someone's back pocket, but for the real benefit of all. You know, Maggie, it's hard not to be pessimistic in this country. Every time a change is contemplated or made, either the media or some special self-interest group or some political hack has to condemn the change before it gets out of the gate. We seem to be challenged by the NDP of this country.

"What's the NDP, Jake?"

"Sorry, Maggie, I should have finished my thought; it is Negative Direction People that whine and moan, because the majority or silent majority of the population doesn't see things their way, or there are those that simply oppose change to oppose change, as they have nothing else to do in life, including work for a living."

"Well, I can see how you think that, given the slow forward progress we are experiencing."

It's good to once again be back home with Katey. It

never seems to matter how often they leave home; when they get home, she just gets so excited to see them, demands their attention for two minutes, and then lies down by their feet, fully sated by their sheer presence, and moves into doggy dreamland.

"Hey, Sweetie, do you remember when I was sitting at the kitchen bar last night and I said that my eyesight has come back to 20/20? I also said that I could see the time on your watch was 9:30 P.M."

"Yes, I do, and I must admit that I am quite amazed at that development."

"Well, hang on to your amazement, Babe, because you are not going to believe this one!"

CHAPTER 12
Missions

The president states, "Gentlemen! Pressure is mounting from all quarters of the informed society, and the U.N. is now seeking explanation as to the nub of the communications idiosyncrasies emanating from Iran. Have any of you around this table garnered further evidence of the nature of the communications block, and/or have you developed a convincing spin that I can flail to those impatient bastards?"

"General Whitmore, sir. We have not confirmed the type or substance relating to the communications failure. We have definitely established that this block only exists over Iranian airspace. Our operatives confirm that there is no visible evidence of anything unusual. Two of our Air Force jets stationed in Iraq have veered one mile into Iran's airspace at its northeast corner, and the pilots have confirmed that they lost communications immediately with base and each other, and several of their navigational instruments were knocked out. Thus far, we conclude that an invisible net of an unknown substance has been suspended over Iran's airspace. This is deduced from the fact that ground communications in Iran are normal and, now, the confirmation that the pilots at twenty thousand feet were without communications. The fact that 'in flow' communications is nonexistent in Iran further confirms this theory. Out flow is mysterious; however, much of the exodus is at ground level, clearly lower than twenty thousand feet. The Pentagon 'Spin Doctors' are working on an Iranian scenario as we speak, sir."

"Good," the president muses, "I want to review that

scenario early tomorrow morning. Who's developing the scenario, General?"

"Captain Pitt, Pentagon Think Tank unit, sir."

"He's a good lad; his father and I spent a lot of time fishing up in Maine and Vermont. I sure miss those days of latching onto a big bass. They were great fighters and a thrill to net them into the boat. Fishing isn't part of the game plan these days given the worldly crisis we are faced with."

"Someday, someday," the President muses. "What's the status of our special covert mission directed toward Iran?"

"Sir, we have now recruited the twenty members of the team. We chose the brightest people with the greatest range of skills and abilities from the widest range of military and secret services in the country. We are assembling this afternoon at the Pentagon to layout collectively the most probable strategic plan of operations. I will be able to brief you this evening or in the morning, your preference, sir."

"That's good, General Whitmore; 06:00 tomorrow is fine with me."

CHAPTER 13
Significant Development

"I noticed a significant change in my vision, Sweetie."

"What's the change, Jake?"

"My left eye sometimes focuses on a distant object and dials that object in as if it were only a few feet away. Man, I just about jumped out of my skin the first time! I was sitting right here looking out toward the apple tree— that's about forty feet, I would guess— then a forward-leaning branch started to ratchet up into closer view. Jesus, I could see a small ant crawling in its usual bazaar manner of meandering."

"Holy crap, Jake, are you for real?"

"I'm not kidding; my eye seems to act as if it were a scope but without the cross hairs— you know similar to my Bushnell 6 – 24 X 40 Scope on my 270 Winchester. It's done it a few times, and I know it isn't my imagination. My eyes feel weird when it happens, with a vibration that tickles the eyeball, and it feels like there is a giant elastic band attached to the back of my cranium, winding up and applying a significant ever-increasing pressure. Weird! My stomach churns and heaves, you know, like when you're about to... Well, you know what I mean."

With a look that suggests "Let me out of here, I'm with a crazy," Maggie says, "I'm so tired; I've just got to go to bed before you turn into a Cyclops! Are you coming, Jake?"

"Yep, I will be there in a jiffy. I just want to try this eye ratcheting one more time, but from a significantly long distance. I think a look at Mount Baker will be just right—

that's about forty miles away— and see what I can zero in on. We have a clear view of Mount Baker from our front bedroom window, and there is still enough light to provide a good test."

"Come, Katey, Jake is standing me up for his new eyeball wizardry. You're a good loyal pup, Katey. You're always here to serve my every need... well almost."

This is truly an unforgettable, fantastic experience, Jake muses to himself. Even with the diminishing light and a slight mist brought about by the cooling air meeting with the warmed ground, Jake can see trees— individual trees— well enough to identify their species. The craggy rock formations, and specifically individual rocks, make this experiment so worthwhile.

Jake can see a couple of hikers on one of the many trails that cris-cross the mountain slope. He begins to wonder if he could spot forest game. Making a slow, methodical sweep of the slope, in and around the many trees and rock outcroppings, Jake believes he has spotted a weasel! In order to confirm the sighting, Jake needs to figure out a way to create a more powerful scope, setting to get a closer look. He focuses his mind on what he is attempting, and his eye zeros in for a closer look. It is a weasel, and it has a good size to it. The mountain environment must be good for it, and its food source must be plentiful given the size of the weasel.

Jake thinks that is an interesting experiment and discovery, noting that the range focusing works so well, so long as he instructs or commands the brain to make the alterations. It isn't rocket science; it's just a normal brain function.

The pressure on the back of Jake's head is about the same as when his eye was zeroing in at about forty feet. That's good to know, Jake thinks. He actually thought it would pull the back of his head through his face. Recognizing no additional pressure difference exists comes as a pleasant surprise.

This has been quite a day. Major developments

have occurred, and one giant leap forward in traversing the parallel universes has been made. Jake, now feeling a bit weary, thinks that bed is a good plan, and besides, Maggie has already warmed the bed.

CHAPTER 14
Chilling Realizations

Maggie wakes up screaming at the top of her lungs. A laser flashes, and the ceiling fan explodes on the beautiful, natural oak hardwood floor.

"Holy Lucifer, Maggie, are you okay!"

Still stunned, Maggie catches her breath and says, "I had an ugly, creepy nightmare; it was so horrible, Jake. I have had horrible nightmares before, but this one... This horrible creature with two oversized heads, eight eyes, and six arms was staring me down and hissing at me on the street in front of our house. I don't know what I was doing out on the front street, but there I was, confronted by this big old, ugly, hideous-looking thing. I ran as fast as my short legs would take me, but I was no match for this nine-foot freaking Goliath. I turned as I ran. Oh, I wish I hadn't. I could see that he or it had a warty, wet skin cover, and he or it was slobbering from his mouth a green bile. It was closing in closer, closer... I stopped dead in my tracks, turned, and to my utter shock and complete surprise, I fired a killer laser beam, blowing it into unrecognizable shards of stinking, reeking, pink, fresh flesh.

"I was totally covered with this warm, wretched-smelling, slimy, sticky green bile. That was bad enough in itself, but then the bile slowly turned into a million little, green maggots, which promptly started to crawl and munch away at my skin. I wished that I were dead. It was horrid, a perfectly horrid experience."

"What happened next, Maggie?"

"I awoke."

"Oh my God, what's happening, Maggie? Come let

me give you a hug. I can sure see you are in dire need for one now. I love you. Our adventurous meeting with Koidon has definitely had an impact on you."

"Oh no, I like Koidon. Besides, he's kind of cute, but maybe my imagination has been just jarred a bit. I can now visualize or believe there are other civilizations that are not so friendly."

"Ain't that the truth!"

"It was a freaking, powerful, dream, Sweetie. When I awoke, Jesus, there was a blinding flash of pure white light. The ceiling fan and light fell to the floor and smashed to smithereens. Holy sheep shit!" Maggie exclaimed.

"Maggie, I think… Don't you stare at anything, please. I think you really did shoot a laser beam or something. The proof is on the floor, and look, the ceiling connector has been burnt off and is still smokin'. Perhaps your dream is forewarning you of the existence of a very hostile environment and to be extra careful while traveling the parallel universes!"

"I think my brain is highly activated and now sensitive to our fuller global environment, and yes, there is an ugly side to all this. There are some realities here that I don't understand, but I know it is somehow connected to our strange experience yesterday or three days ago or whenever. I don't know anymore."

"Careful with your eyes, Babe, they're deadly. Goodnight!"

"Goodnight, Jake."

"Good morning Sweetie! Its' now time to get up."

Jake breaks out in a song he heard on the radio long ago.

Wake up, wake up you sleepy head; get your little buns out of bed.

"Oh Jake, my darling, how can you be so happy and alive at this God given hour? I can barely get one eye open."

66

"Open the other eye very carefully, please… I'm a morning person, Babe. I will put on the coffee, grab the paper, and see who shot whom!

The early morning hour prior to Maggie's rusing is a special time for Jake. Jake delights in capturing the news headlines but is often sickened by the actions of some killing and maiming others for their own lust for power and greed. Jake figures that the demise in civil behavior is primarily the result of liberal attitudes toward such behavior, such as a catch and release program within the so-called justice system.

Jake thinks while rolling his eyes, "Only in Canada, *eh*!"

Jake turns on the TV and, by accident selects, a foreign language station. Jake listens, and he soon realizes that he is beginning to understand what is being said. He listens with more intent and now is becoming quite comfortable with his overall comprehension of the language. Jake then tunes into a French language station, and after a few minutes he, becomes comfortable with understanding that language, too. Jake is amazed at how his evolution is occurring and realizes just how important this newly acquired skill will benefit him in the future.

"Jesus, Jake," Maggie exclaims. "I just discovered that I can ratchet my right eye to bring objects closer, like you. It's truly amazing. I now understand the feelings you had last night, as I have now experienced them as well. I am so-o-o-o sorry for thinking you were going to become a Cyclops. Now we both are, and that's not so bad really. Maybe I was just a little jealous of your developments, Jake. I also observed numbers tripping over as I was zooming in. I am sure it is telling me the actual distance. You didn't mention that fact to me, Jake."

"You're right, because I haven't experienced that. I find it quite odd that we aren't developing the skills in the same way."

"It's just human nature for growth and development to occur at our own individual speed, Jake. My brain is not yours, and thank God it isn't, because you think up some pretty weird stuff, and your interests are different from mine. Besides, I am a woman, in case you haven't noticed lately. In the end I believe we will share similar skills."

"Hey Babe, you always have a good answer for everything, and believe me: I never forget you are a woman. I guess the reason I can't fire laser bursts from my eyes is because I'm not a fiery redhead."

"You mind your tongue, Jake. You're on dangerous ground; ya hear? You wouldn't want me to look at you the wrong way; would ya?"

"No, no, no. Just recognizing that there are differences. See I get it. I liked your response."

"Pass the toll, Jake. Kiss and make-up."

"Hey, Sweetie, the coffee is ready; the paper is here; and Katey is outside. I think I would like to spend the next hour just having a good old familiar breakfast, complete a crossword puzzle and do a Sudoku. Oh yes, just like I used to do."

"That idea sounds warm and entertaining to me, Jake.

"We do need to make further progress today; we just can't loll. Something is driving me and, as sure that I am alive, I still don't know what it is."

"I know, Sweetie," Maggie says. "Sometimes answers come to you rather than you running after them"

"True enough, Maggie, although something is pushing me in an exploring direction. Maybe it is Dad dropping a hint or a clue?"

"Jake, you have to go with your intuition. So, whatever you want to do, I am with you."

"Thanks, Sweetie, I need all the support I can get, and I am happy it is you. We have traveled several parallel universes now, and we know we have friends and potential support in Koidon and his civilization in Naranna. They have special powers, it seems, and these powers may be useful to us in the future. I would like to return to Naranna soon, but not today. I have other urges."

"Jake, can you let Katey in, please."

"Yep... Hi, Katey Girl, did you have a fun time chasing the squirrels? Come on in. It's breakfast time for you, too. I'll get you your food and water. Good Pup.... Maggie, I have a strong feeling that we need to go to Washington D.C."

"Why Washington, D.C., Jake?"

"I have a sense that some very important discussions are taking place at the White House that will assist us in understanding what the purpose of our mission is."

"Your Dad is talking to you; isn't he?

"He is, but he isn't talking to me directly, just dropping whole pieces of bread this time. Wow! The urge to go is immense and growing. I even have a pain in my groin; it's been awhile."

"Maybe tonight, Jake, so long as you don't completely wear me out today. You know, I'm not as young, as I once was."

"Maggie, somehow we have to find a split or overlapping universe so we can attend those discussions without detection. Do you have any thoughts on how we achieve that feat?"

"Hmm. At the moment, I don't. Jake, just how do you think we are going to get to Washington?"

"I just thought we could step through a portal and arrive there."

"We have not done that before, Jake. What we have been doing is slipping into parallel universes. It's different this time; we are staying within our own universe and simply teleporting ourselves to Washington."

"Okay Maggie, I see where you are coming from, and we have yet to develop that skill. I know that teleporting is possible, because Koidon uses that method to travel through his universe. Jesus, we can't take a plane as we don't have that amount of time. I need to think."

"I'll think hard too, Jake."

Over a couple of cups of coffee, half a naval orange,

69

and two pieces of whole grain toast, Maggie and Jake go into their own solitudes. There is a deathly silence in the air that makes Katey feel very uncomfortable. Katey is not used to this type of silence and is fearful that her masters are about to abandon her in favor of more travels to where ever they go.

"Maggie, I think I got it. I just remembered my conversation about teleportation with Koidon. He said, 'It is simply mind over matter.' Let's go, Maggie. I just need to get my backpack and get the guns out of the locked storage cabinet. On second thought, I will leave the guns at home. We will likely appear in Washington in full view of the public, so it wouldn't be cool carrying guns."

"Okay, Jake, I'm ready to go. Bye, Katey, we will be home in a little while; we promise."

"Hold, my hand, Maggie. Let's both focus our minds' attention on Washington, D.C."

After a couple of minutes, Jake and Maggie simply disappear from the living room where they stand. They re-appear across the street from the White House in Washington. While the sidewalk is awash with people scurrying in all different directions, their arrival seems to go without notice. That's the way life is. In a busy urban center, people just keep to themselves and mind their own business. One would think if people just appeared out of nowhere, there would be a little shock or cry of dismay or something, but not in this case. It's as though they have their blinders on and are hell-bent to get to wherever they are going. Perhaps they realize that it is better to let sleeping dogs lie; don't get involved; just mind your own business; life is tough enough just surviving the urban jungle. Who needs to mess with fate?

"How did you figure out teleportation, Jake?"

"It just came to me as we were thinking hard. If its mind over matter, which it really is, then I thought if I pinpoint the coordinates, i.e. the latitude and the longitude, we might get lucky, and we did."

"So how did you know the coordinates? You have

never been that good with geography."

"Good question, Maggie. They just came to me and I didn't question them. I guess I have acquired another skill, Navigation and maybe an improvement in geograpy, too. Okay, Sweetie, now it's your turn. We want to end up in the presidential meeting room. Have you mastered entering a split or overlapping universe?"

"I think I can do it, but don't ask for any explanation just yet."

"Okay, we don't have time right now. Anyway, its one o'clock local time, and the meeting is about to start."

"Hold my hand, Jake; I'm going to give this a try."

Like taking a half-step, they enter the meeting room. Mindful of their being, they steer clear of those who are gathering. Observation is their mission, and they do not want anything to go wrong. The president walks in and sits down. The other members are now already seated.

CHAPTER 15
Prognostication

"Mr. President, Major Pitt, Think Tank unit, Pentagon, requests entry for briefing."

"Bradley, a great pleasure to see you; how's your dad?"

"Good, he's gone fishing as usual, sir. That's his life."

"Good! Good! Briefly, what are your prognostications?"

"Sir, two weeks ago, two unidentified objects appeared in space. We have been observing them and trying to identify the origin of these objects. So far we have determined the objects are created from a manmade source."

"How do you know that for sure?" the president, queries.

"Sir, we had the Hubble telescope take a specific look at them. It reported back that they are very similar satellites orbiting in space. Material identification indicates that they're made of earthly products. The exterior appendages such as antenna, radar, and solar screens are similar to those globally manufactured. One major difference in the suspected objects is their shape; however, we believe this is to foil identification rather than to have any other significance."

"What shape are these objects?" the president asks.

"Sir, these objects are shaped like a long cylinder with small wing-like stabilizers as well as the usual exterior hardware found on most satellites. While have not identified the source of the objects, we do believe it is some kind of a communication device; however, we have not detected any source of transmission or receipt of data. We have been watching them closely and, up to now, they appear not to be activated. The orbital positioning of these satellites and excessive distance from Earth are odd, sir. From our intelligence, we do not believe Iran has developed a super communication blocking type of weapon. They haven't figured out the atomic bomb. The sophisticated technical requirements would be well beyond them, sir. We haven't continued our development of such weaponry as the rest of the world has, and our own national policy has been specific toward a non-military approach to space. International agreements are currently in place without knowledgeable breach. The U.N. is not aware of any recent launches of satellites, nor has it given any approvals. Whoever launched these devices is clearly in contravention to established protocols and agreements."

"Major Pitt," the president asks, "do you think these two objects have anything to do with the dilemma we face, and if so, what are your thoughts?"

"Sir, we cannot comprehend a net being suspended over Iran. Our fighter pilots encountered communications loss while flying over Iran at twenty thousand feet."

At that moment, tired of standing, Jake and Maggie decide to sit in the two vacant chairs and, in doing so, walk past a few of the committee members, including the president.

The president stops the meeting and states, "Is it just me, or is anyone else feeling a little uncomfortable?"

General Whitmore speaks up. "Mr. President, just a moment ago, I felt a rush of air, as if someone had just walked past me. I also have this eerie sense of feeling that someone is watching us."

The president states, "I have the same uncomfortable, eerie feeling. I don't believe in ghosts; however, before we continue this meeting, I will have security come in and use the infrared scanners and heat detectors to ensure our security. The issue we are dealing with simply cannot leak out. We can never be too careful."

A White House Security Team arrives at the meeting room and requests that everyone leave the room and wait in the hall.

"This should only take about ten minuets, Mr. President."

Maggie and Jake also walk out into the hall and steer clear of the others waiting patiently.

"The room is safe to re-enter. We did not detect any infiltration: humans, spirits, video, bugs, or any other device."

"Thanks, we can resume this meeting."

Everyone re-enters the room, including Jake and Maggie. Jake and Maggie look at each other and give each other a happy, winning smile. This being their first occasion in an overlapping universe, they dare not speak to each other nor risk other activities simply because they cannot anticipate the impact.

The president addresses the meeting attendees. "Gentlemen order. Major Pitt, please continue."

"Sir, I will repeat my last comment in order to maintain the context: Sir, we cannot comprehend a net being suspended over Iran. Our fighter pilots encountered communications loss while flying over Iran at twenty thousand feet. This suggests to us that the communication net is being transmitted rather than suspended. Sir, perhaps these two objects are transmitting the block over Iran. Their distance from Earth and their elliptical orbit suggest to us it is possible for these two objects to never lose view of Iran. This is purely speculative. We just don't know, and frankly, sir, we still think they are dormant, that is unless they have somehow developed a completely foreign type of technology from that of our existing transmitting methodology. We see this as a possible scenario, and we are attempting to communicate with these objects and further our investigation with our closest satellites. We are quite baffled at these objects' sudden appearance in space. All the recording tapes at our disposal have been revisited, and we have determined no recorded history of their launch or the establishment of their orbit. It is only conceivable that Russia or China could possibly have developed such a new technology, given the knowledge base they are drawing from, as they are considered world leaders in space development, as we are, sir. If they are involved, that would be in violation of the world's space agreement not to use space for military purposes. We don't believe, given the current good relationships that we have with these countries, that they can be held accountable without specific proof."

"Major Pitt, rule number one: You do not *assume* anything. Sometimes what seems not to be is true. Keep working on that theory."

"Yes, sir"

"General Whitmore, since we are now armed with this additional information, why don't we focus this spin around Iran and Korea with the atomic bomb twist?"

"You make a good point, Mr. President. We're on it."

"General Whitmore, an update on our Iranian mission is urgently needed."

"We have determined the targets that we will search and have a general game plan in place. It appears that ground communications are okay, so we intend to infiltrate Iran below radar height at 22:00 hours and enter the country at six entry points. The operation is estimated to take a maximum of six hours inside Iran once our mission has been initiated. We estimate our approach will enhance our success and survival rate by forty percent, sir."

"Good update, and may God be with you all, as your mission is for the good of all. Meeting adjourned."

As the president is leaving the meeting room, he is once again overcome with this uncomfortable, eerie feeling that someone is watching him. He turns around slowly and studies those left in the room and the vacant spaces, looking for some clue of a strange presence, but none is apparent.

"Are you alright, Mr. President?" asks General Whitmore.

"Yes, General, but that strange feeling has come over me again. Maybe I'm just tired. I don't know."

"Mr. President, just remember you were not the only one experiencing what you were experiencing. There was a presence. I know I, too, felt its presence. Of what it was, I just don't know, sir. I don't like it, but it appears we are unable to deal with it right now."

Jake and Maggie leave the room the same way that they recently entered and arrive out in front of the White House, where they initially started from.

"Wow!" says Jake. "That was an incredible trip, Sweetie, and I think we just got the sense of our mission."

"Holy sheep shit, Jake!

"I couldn't believe it when the president stopped the meeting. What a dumb look on his face! And I truly think he was in near panic."

"I agree. It was pretty funny, and they had no clue as to what they were experiencing. Do you think we would have been detected by heat sensors or infrared scanners?"

"I don't know, Maggie. I have never had any experience with them. So, Maggie would you like to find a bar and have a glass of wine or two."

"No, Jake, I just want to get back home safe and sound and see Katey."

"Hold my hand, Maggie. If all goes right, we should be home in a second or so."

Jake and Maggie simply materialize in their own living room, completely intact and feeling very smitten about the day's achievements.

"Hi, Katey. How's my girl? Did you miss us? How would you like a short walk of wonderful scents?"

With an offer like that, Katey races to the partially closed closet, grabs her leash, and sits in front of Maggie, impatiently nudging her, wanting her to hurry up and open the door.

"Oh Jake, I will have that glass of wine with you

when I get back."

"Okay", Jake says, and with that, Maggie and Katey head out for their walk.

While Maggie and Katey are out, Jake replays the day's events. The mere thought that the Americans are currently stumped in resolving what appears to be a serious and dangerous game someone or some country is playing— and, for what end?— puzzles him. Jake has a lot of questions in his head as to what he has just heard and begins wondering how they themselves can be helpful in the resolution.

He smugly smiles to himself, thinking about the timely manner in which his and Maggie's new skills have developed on a demand basis. He thinks how incredible their brain growth and development has been and how fortunate they are to have been chosen for this huge task. Maybe he shouldn't be so smug, he thinks. It isn't coincidental; it was planned after all. His memory is now jogged. This new-found talent and ability was likely a gift to them from the Higher Power, giving new meaning to the gravity of this crisis and perhaps a supernatural response requirement needed. Maggie and Katey return, and with one look at Katey, you know she is well-sated with the neighborhood's variety of wonderful scents. Over a glass of wine for Maggie and a glass of good scotch for Jake, they recall the events of the day. Maggie has surprised herself with her new-found ability to seek out and find portals for split universes. She also thinks that it was fun to be in that environment, knowing that she could observe others and obtain information without detection. She also feels uneasy that it is possible to carry out such a feat and, in essence, become a spy and betray peoples trust; however, she thinks, what the hell; it is for the good of all.

Jake is also proud of his achievements with regard to achieving teleportation. He is more relieved than ever that they are able to do what they did and return safely.

"Maggie, I have a strong sense that we opened a major door today. Cheers!"

CHAPTER 16
More to Seek

Another day dawns and Jake is already up and planning the days, activities. Maggie and Katey are still asleep. The smell of freshly brewed Kona coffee wafts throughout the house. A morning without coffee is like a dark, dank, gray day teaming with chilly Vancouver West Coast rain.

Jake is pondering a number of options in his head. Russia and China seem like possibilities to consider slipping into. Then, there is the return to Naranna. Jake considers the biggest payoff would likely be Russia, although he would prefer to go to Naranna, a familiar and delightful place. The Russians have been in the space program a lot longer than China and likely pose a greater threat, given the air is a little chilly between the U.S. and Russia over the European Defense System. A quiet visit to their space center might prove interesting.

"Hi, Katey. Is mom up, too?"

"Yes, I am up but not awake," Maggie croaks out. "You wore me out yesterday traipsing all over the country; I would love to just sit and put my feet up and read a good book."

"Sorry, honey, can't loll today. I have this urge again."

"You know what I would love? To lead a normal life. But, if you have an urge and a mission in mind you know that I am always with you."

"Thanks, Sweetie. The mission today is to visit the Russian space facilities. I think it is a good bet, given the fact that Russia is likely number two in the space race."

"Okay, I'm on, but I can't without breakfast."

"Oh, of course food is a necessity. I'm not in that big of a hurry, as I haven't read my paper or done a crossword puzzle and a Sudoku yet."

"Jake, do you think it would be worthwhile to visit your dad again, just to touch base and gain a sense of what he is thinking about our progress."

"Yeah, I have been thinking about that, too. As a matter of fact, that very thought occurred to me this morning."

"Well, aren't we on the same page, Jake?"

"Amazing, utterly amazing, Maggie, but then again that's why I married you. We are always on the same page."

"What, not for my good looks or my sexy body?"

"Sweetie, remember when we first met, we agreed: friends first, intellectual compatibility second, and then the body, which includes the external looks. You're looking absolutely smashing."

"That's what I love about you, Jake: You always know how to make a girl feel good, and you are never a threat, not to mention all your positive support and compassion you give me. I have always said, 'Where has this man been all my life?' as you are not like most men, I have known. You are not afraid to show your emotions nor afraid to get closer to me when I am in distress or suffering from anxiety or fear or even crying a little or maybe a lot."

"Thanks, Sweetie, I really do love you, Maggie, and I can't imagine life without you. I'm opting to go to Russia today, and maybe tomorrow we can visit Dad again. Are you okay with that, Maggie?"

"I'm with you, Babe... Breakfast was good, oh so good and filling, so now I am ready to go, Jake."

"Okay, Maggie. I'll get my pack and, again, leave my guns at home. I think it would be a good idea if we take our passports with us today. After all, we will be visible for some period of time in a truly foreign country."

"Good thinking, Jake. It would never have occurred

to me that we would need a passport."

"Hold my hand Maggie. We need to think about the coordinates for Omsk."

"Where is Omsk and why there, Jake?"

"Omsk is an obscure village in Siberia, which I have reason to believe is one of Russia's best kept secrets when it comes to covert space operations and forward developing defense developments and technologies. The Ruskies don't tell the Americans everything, you know."

"For what I think we are looking for, we have a better chance in Omsk than St. Petersburg, Leningrad, or Moscow. Besides I think I received a clue that we should follow."

In a few minutes, Jake and Maggie disappear from their living room and appear in the town of Omsk.

"Wow! Quite a modern community in what appears to be the middle of nowhere. Maggie, I sense that, by our clothing, we stand out. I have seen a number of people eye us so strangely, as if we were aliens. I think we should get a move on toward our destination and be quick about it."

"Good thought Jake."

"Jesus, I thought there might be some clue as to where there are facilities, but there doesn't appear to be any military operations here."

Maggie and Jake wander the streets and the outskirts of Omsk, looking for some evidence to suggest a military presence. In the northwest quadrant of the community, a couple of luxury-looking vehicles emerge from nowhere that is evident. Maggie and Jake kneel down behind some bushes for cover and to observe covertly the two vehicles as they pass by. The first vehicle contains four men, all dressed in similar fashion. Although the windows are tinted and it is difficult to obtain a clear vision, their guess is that they are military or at least police in uniform. The second vehicle contains a driver donning similar attire while a graying and balding man in the rear seat appears to be a civilian. Jake makes the assumption that the gentleman in the rear seat of the second car is a scientist by his demeanor.

"Maggie, I am curious as to where those vehicles came from. Let's see what we can find."

As Jake and Maggie once again begin to move in the direction where the vehicles have come from, three additional vehicles appears.

Maggie blurts out, "Hide Jake! It doesn't make sense that they instantly appear Jake. There must be a drop off or some other obscure entry beyond our sight. I have engaged my telescopic vision but only see hillsides."

"You're onto something, Maggie. We need to get a closer look, but there is no cover for us."

"Oh yes there is Jake. We only need to find a split universe, and I will take on that task.

Jake and Maggie hold hands and vanish from their hiding place. After a few moments, they find themselves in an obscure corner of a very large building complex. There are no windows to be seen, and the ceiling is made up of a very complex mix of lights. The light intensity makes them feel as if they are outside. A hum of electricity exists in the air, but no life is evident from this vantage point.

"Where do you think we are, Maggie?"

"I don't know, but I sense we are in an underground bunker, perhaps in the power plant."

"Hmm, good thought, Maggie. Perhaps we should explore. Chances are we will not be detected unless this place is outfitted with infrared sensors."

Jake and Maggie realize that they are in a vast underground facility. It is an underground hydro-power plant that they are in, and it connects to a maze of underground tunnels. Taking what they presume is the main tunnel; they walk for about fifty minutes before observing some people riding a tram. They quickly hide behind some old rusting barrels and are not detected. Maggie thinks that following the tram would lead them to some business activities.

Jake suddenly realizes that it is not necessary to hide, because they are in a split universe, and he suggests that they run after the tram and secure some seats in the rear. There are observed vacancies.

Not much energy is exerted to catch the tram, as it is traveling quite slowly. Once seated on the tram they, begin listening in on some of the interesting conversations, none of which seem to be of the subject matter that they have come to hear. The tram pulls up to a stop in front of a set of very large doors. All of the tram's patrons disembark the tram, so Maggie and Jake think it prudent that they do the same. Following the workers through the huge doors, they enter a very large room filled with equipment and a maze of frozen pipes, as well as an equal number of pipes that are steaming hot. They conclude that this is just an extension of the power plant and that this is where the facilities were being monitored.

"Maggie, this isn't getting us anywhere; can you see if you can land us somewhere that has a little more excitement and relevance to the success of our mission?"

"Jake, you are making it difficult for me. You didn't do enough research."

"Sorry, Sweetie, I will do better next time."

"I forgive you, Jake. Hold my hand, Jake" she says, and in a few minutes, they find themselves in a huge building, which turns out to be the control center of the Russian space program. One room is as big as a football stadium, with a thousand cubical desks on the main floor portion. Those people are manning computers, and at this moment, Jake and Maggie can only conclude that they are keeping track of their many satellites. At the front of this room is a complete bank of monitors and the photos that are coming up are awesome.

After wandering around in this room and listening in on the local conversations, they decide that this is not the right place either.

"Okay, Maggie, how about one more kick at the can."

"Okay, Jake. Hold onto my hand and hang on."

In a couple of minutes they find themselves in a

science lab, where about five hundred people are busy working away on a variety of projects.

Ah, thinks Jake, this looks promising. Jake and Maggie wander from station to station, perking their ears up to ensure their ability to listen in on conversations.

Two very officious-looking scientists are discussing the shield over Iran and are in a heated debate as to what is causing such a phenomenon. The older scientist (they observe the name Boris on his nametag) is suggesting that the shield is being beamed down from a satellite; however, he was unable to come to any definitive conclusion as to which satellite is the culprit.

The younger scientist dismisses this notion and suggests that Iran is broadcasting a wide beam that is blanketing Iran's air space. He suggests that it is not electro-magnetic; rather it is using plasma infusion and forcing its delivery via a mix of long and short wave radio signals. This mixing accelerates the neutrons, thereby creating an impregnable web. It is similar to creating mass confusion between the waves, resulting in total distortion of any communication signal.

Jake says to Maggie, "It doesn't sound like Russia has anything to do with this shield, as they seem to be somewhat dismayed at its presence. They, too, have no solution but are obviously investing time to solve this very important issue."

Jake and Maggie move on toward another station that displays a number of large visual displays. As they turn the corner and head toward the next station, sirens and red flashing lights fired up with a certain velocity. Maggie immediately notices their image showing up on one of the large screens. While the images are somewhat vague, they definitely depict them.

"Oh my God," Maggie blurts out in total horror. "We have been had. Look at the left screen, Jake!"

"Holy crap, let's get out of this corridor. It's likely monitored by infrared rays, and we just triggered it."

"Jesus, Jake, a hoard of armed men are rushing

toward us."

"Quick, Maggie, take a quick turn left, then right and right again, and let's hide in this vacant office. We will never get out of this building through conventional methods Maggie. Can you get us back home or even back out onto the street where we first entered the buildings."

The soldiers sense their presence in the vacant office and try to open the door. Fumbling with the keys, attempting to locate the right key, one impatient officer smashes the door window.

"I'm on it Jake. Hold my hand."

"Hurry, Maggie. The jig is up."

Just as the soldiers enter the room... poof... Maggie and Jake make a soft and safe landing in the living room of their own home.

"Jesus, Maggie, I owe you one. When did you master the art of teleportation?"

"Just now. Pretty good work, don't you think?"

"I'm so impressed. Let me pour you a nice glass of white wine. I think I will treat myself to a nice scotch, single malt even." Jake thinks for a moment. "I have such a forest of scotch to choose from, maybe this calls for a twenty-five-year-old Scotch, Highland Park. Yes, a good choice, given we made it home safely... It's unusual for Katey not to be standing in front of the glass door wanting to welcome us home. I think I had better have a quick look to see if everything is okay, Maggie... There you are, Katey. Are you too tired to get out of your bed or just not feeling too well today. I love that wanting look on your face, but frankly, it pains me to see you this way.

"Jake, I am afraid we are nearing the time for discussions about Katey."

"I know. Let's see how she is in the morning and we will make a decision as to whether she can make the trip with us or maybe a trip to the veterinarian will be necessary."

CHAPTER 17
Help!

"Good Morning, Sweetie! I see Katey is a little low this morning, so today would be a good day to visit Dad. You want to come with me?"

"I would love to see your dad again but not today. I'm sorry. Katey is not all that perky, and I think I would like to spend some good, quality time with her. Besides, I just need a good stay-at-home day to get caught up on things around here and get some rest. You have been wearing me out lately, but not in that good old, fun, bed-romping way. Jake, you need some good, quality time with your dad, and alone would be the best way to accomplish that."

"I hear you, Maggie, and I agree you are right. I'm going to miss you today. Give me a kiss and a hug, Maggie, as I am on my way."

Jake goes upstairs into the bedroom, thinking how he can make the best out of meeting with his dad. So much has occurred in recent weeks that it is becoming increasingly difficult to just live a normal life. It is fun and full of adventure trying to carry out this unknown mission for the good of all, but a normal life would be good, too.

Jake knows Maggie is wearing a little thin and is yearning to have him to herself once again to make love, walk on the beach, go on picnics, or just spend time in the back yard mowing the grass or pulling weeds. A movie would be good and so would a nice quiet, romantic, moonlit dinner, overlooking the ocean. Yes, life was bliss and he yearns for the return of the days before the vog swept them off the East Beach of Semiahmoo Bay.

Jake slaps himself in the face as a reminder that important things lie ahead and there will be plenty of time in the future, when this mission is complete, to gorge on the delights that nature has bestows on them as fortunate humans. Now it is time for him to see his dad.

Jake turns to face the south wall as he remembers Maggie has once done and reaches up to feel for the port to Meadowbrook. This is Jake's first attempt, and he is feeling good that perhaps he, too, has developed the skill to enter a parallel universe. Having found the port, Jake takes a small step forward and slips into a very black, lonely hole.

Oh my God, where in Sam Hell am I going? Jake thinks. Sheer panic overcomes Jake as he is being propelled deeper and deeper into this black, lonely hole of nothingness.

Having never experienced total darkness except once in a cave at the Craters of the Moon in Idaho, Jake's stomach starts to roll and heave. His sense of balance is long gone, and frankly, he doesn't know the difference between up or down. Lost in this black hole, definitely moving and tumbling uncontrollably is not my idea of fun, Jake thinks. Is this my fate? Will I see my darling Maggie again? What in Hell's Bells have I done?

It seems like a lifetime for Jake, traveling in, circling or meandering through this black hole. Jake's whole life passes before him in a flash, and he suddenly catches himself smiling as the many wonderful memories are instantly recanted.

Jake, for the moment, has forgotten his panic and is beginning to feel somewhat more comfortable in his new environment. After all, he feels no pain; he is still alive; he feels all over his body; and it is all there, thank God. One's manhood is of utmost importance?

Something catches his attention, bringing him back to the reality of his situation. The air is getting cooler and a soft cool wind breezes past his face. A moment ago, there was nothing, perhaps like being a sardine in a vacuum-sealed tin. But, there is something. The environment is quickly changing. Emerging ubiquitously, creaks, groans, and shrieks of an unearthly sort are building, growing into a greater din.

Jake no longer feels that he is moving in or circling through this black hole. Eerily, still, in this not-so-nice environment, Jake is feeling a little unruffled and apprehensive, anticipating what might lie before him. It's the not knowing that is especially difficult to deal with, and he can now feel his heart starting to pump and race with anticipation. Perspiration begins to bead on his face, and his body instantly shivers uncontrollably as his fears begin to build to a climax. Jesus, it's so dark, cold, and creepy, he thinks, and not being able to see anything begins a blood draining and energy zapping process in Jake's mind.

Just as quickly as Jake had entered the dark lonely black hole, the black hole light suddenly flickers on. Holy shit, Jake thought! What the hell gives, no environment exists that is dark one second and then brilliantly lit the next second, it just doesn't make sense to him. This must be some form of an artificial environment. This scares the shit out him not understanding where he is or what he has gotten myself into.

Jake emerges from the dark only to find himself in a rugged countryside completely devoid of vegetation. The ground beneath his feet is made up of gritty, course sand and small wind-eroded pebbles. The hillsides are filled with hoodoos towering some fifty to one hundred feet in height. Jake thinks that this area must suffer from some fierce windstorms to create the soil erosion that has taken place here. Today, the air is calm, and he senses that it is all that is calm as a chill creeps up his tingling spine.

Meanwhile, Maggie is busy in the house, dusting, vacuuming, washing the mound of dirty dishes, and staring at the mounds of dirty clothes awaiting her attention. Jesus, I really need a maid, she thinks. This housework just sucks when you live the fast-paced life that I now find myself living.

Maggie turns her attention to Katey; she seems to

be feeling much better now, and she even wants her belly rubbed. Maggie can't stop thinking of all the good times she has had with Katey and begins to weep just thinking that she is about to leave this world, this assignment and perhaps bring happiness to someone else in another life. The mere fact that they only lease or rent these animals or borrow them for such a short while is saddening. They bring with them so much happiness, joy, love, unconditional love, loyalty, another heartbeat in the house, and they sense your every mood and respond to you accordingly.

Maggie's mind wanders over to Jake. Hoping he is all right and having a good meeting with his dad, she begins to feel bad that she has selfishly decided to stay home today, but at the time that Jake wanted to go, she felt so overwhelmed with what lay before her in the house and was deeply concerned over Katey's condition. She knew that, if she didn't take the bull by the horns, the work around the house would never get done. Jake is so focused on his mission that he overlooks the squalor that their home has become; he doesn't notice it anymore.

God, I just want to get my old life back, she thinks. Life was so wonderful, serendipitous even. Everything was going our way— a nice house in a wonderful location, a loving husband, a noble beautiful dog, good friends, neighbors, and family, and a very comfortable life style. What else could anyone want, she thinks.

Suddenly, she becomes overwhelmed with the thought and her realization that everyone needs a solid purpose in life. A bit of adventure is good to keep you young, but all the more important is the feeling of doing something that will benefit others and provide a better world for them to live in.

That's it, she thinks, our mission is just that. The importance of being successful or just trying our best unselfishly is what matters and makes us even better human beings. That's what life is all about for Koidon and his people, and that's what life should be for us humans, she thinks. Oh, I feel better already, and now I wish that I had gone with Jake. Some partner I am, she shrugs.

Maggie strokes Katey. While Katey is resting her head on Maggie's lap, Maggie begins sensing that not all is well with Jake. A strange paranormal sensation goes through Maggie's spine and goose bumps appear all over her body. She breaks out in a cold sweat as her mind keeps telling her, "Jake needs me now!" She can feel his pain and anguish. The pain in her stomach is sharp and piercing. "Oh God, why am I not there with my darling husband?"

Jake decides he will explore this wild and rugged environment for awhile to see if he can find anything useful for fulfilling his mission. Venturing out and onto a flat plain, Jake soon feels that what he is walking on what was once an ocean. The ground is very sandy, and there is minute evidence of the remains of shellfish. Jake reaches down and scoops up a bit of sand and then tastes it; the sand is salty, as he would expect an ocean to be.

What ever happened here will likely remain a mystery. Was the drying up of this ocean the result of global warming, or did the ground just open up and suck the water in? Where is this place? Is it Earth, another planet, or another solar system? Jake cannot recall ever seeing a place so ugly, barren, or inhuman before, except for while viewing photos of the Moon or of Mars. Could this be Annaran, the past planet once inhabited by Koidon? He mentioned that the water disappeared into the earth. Koidon also mentioned the existence of very treacherous civilizations. Who knows where he is. All he really knows is that this place is nasty, and he wishes that he never came here. There is no sign of life forms, but noises— whirring noises, grunts and groans, and, every once in a while, blood curdling screams— broadcast over the horizon, making Jake's hair stand on end.

Jake's heart stops in a flash. There are two nine-foot, giant-sized creatures with two heads and six arms rapidly approaching him. He focuses his telescopic eye on the two approaching him to gain a firmer identification.

"Oh shit," Jake panics. "They are similar to the one that Maggie dreamed about chasing her down our front street, and then, she eye-laser-beamed it, but in reality, she laser-beam-burned off the bedroom ceiling light fixture. Is this sighting a coincidence, or is it the reality of Maggie's dream as a foretold omen." As they are nearing Jake, he began to feel the ground beneath his feet shudder and quake. A sickening feeling overcomes him.

Fearing for his life, but held there in a menacing, trance, forbidding terror races through his mind. From out of the crusty ground bursts eels, huge eels with bodies a circumference of dinner plates— about eight inches— and a length of about ten feet. About twenty of these creatures, with their razor sharp teeth, ferociously attack these freaking two-headed monsters and savagely bite them to death. Death-defying screams echo through the air while the sight and smell of blood, gore, and torn flesh churn Jake's stomach, bringing him to the edge of puking.

A freaking, horrid, frightening sight it is; however, Jake is just thanking his lucky stars that the eels have gotten those freaking monsters before they got him. Jettisoned from his trance, he can feel the ground under his feet becoming more unstable, rumbling and quaking hard, and as Jake turns to run, another eel-like monster bursts through the crusty ground and grabs Jake's right leg, digging deeply with its razor sharp teeth, inflicting immense pain, and blood gushes profusely.

Biting down harder and harder, Jake screams from the excruciating pain, and thinking of his imminent demise, he turns his head and faces this attacking eel. Shocking himself, he shoots a bolt of white laser light from his eyes. Zap! The eel slumps to the ground all afire and certainly dead. Jake rips off the right arm of his shirt and quickly wraps and ties it around his ugly wound.

Jake realizes that he is still in imminent danger and has to get off this dried up ocean bed, so he opts for levitation to get him to safer ground and in a hurry.

90

Jake is ever so surprised and smitten over the fact that levitation actually works, as this is the first time he has tried out this skill.

Having spied these freaking two-headed giants, Jake knows he has entered a very bad portal and now directs his energies to get out of this hole. Jake makes it to where he figures it always to have been dry land and throws himself to the ground, rolling over clutching his right leg in the hopes of easing the intense pain. He looks up toward the sky and gets another surprise. A flock of bird-like creatures, which is nearly invisible except for the creatures' bold, ebony, beady eyes, is hovering overhead and making a weird noise. Assuming they are birds, he studies their behavior and frantically searches for other clues so he can identify them. At times, a shadowy outlines form, giving the bird-like creatures some specific definition; however, as fast as the outlines appear, they disappears. Resonating from the creatures is an eerie sound that Jake thinks sounds like "whir-bet". It echoes and becomes louder or softer as the flock moves. A strange sight to behold, Jake isn't sure if they are waiting for him to die or if they hold other significant meaning. The creatures do not appear threatening.

The creatures— or, as Jake has named them, "whir-bits"— start to roll in mid-air and head inland, then turn back toward Jake, repeating the same maneuver, a maneuver Jake has seen so often and loves, as he has often witnessed the Blue Angels and Snowbirds at Air Shows execute them so gracefully. Jake thinks that they are trying to communicate with him, wanting him to follow them further inland. Having moved another fifty feet inland and being partially obscured from shore, Jake turns back, shocked to see the shore crawling with what appears to be giant, snapping sea turtles. He looks up toward the flock of mysterious bird-like creatures and smiles a big "thank you".

Jesus, Jesus, Jesus, I have to get out of here now; but how? I broke a rule, Jake thinks. I didn't take the time to fully understand my newly acquired skill, and I had been warned.

Jake not only didn't take the time to fully understand the skill, but he didn't know if he possessed the capability of slipping through to a parallel universe. He just took it for granted that, if Maggie could achieve such a feat, he could simply do the same— a brash attitude at best that could result in undesirable ends, and it did.

Jake begins thinking about what combination of skills is required in order to achieve entry to a parallel universe. While he defines Meadowbrook as his destination, he has yet to consult his navigational tools or his sense of "does this feel right?" Jake is determined to get it right and engages all of what he thinks is necessary to engage to facilitate his arrival in Meadowbrook, so he engages his brain into overdrive to ensure that his past mistake is not repeated. He also thinks that, if he doesn't get out of this God-forsaken place soon, he may never get out.

The wind starts to pick up and associated with the wind is an icy, bone-chattering chill. Feeling very cold, Jake again focuses his attention on getting to Meadowbrook and this time achieves his goal.

Standing on the pearly white sandy beach of Lake Eden in Meadowbrook, Jake stands stunned, agog, relieved, and thankful that something or someone is truly looking out for him. To be in Meadowbrook means the world to Jake, for he now knows that he will again see his beautiful wife. He has been given another chance in life.

Jake spots his dad in the distance as he approaches with a big, broad smile on his deeply tanned face, and he appears genuinely happy and proud to see him. They sit on a nearby bench, taking advantage of the scenic view of Lake Eden and the pastoral countryside that surrounds.

His dad looks at the wound on Jake's right calf and states, "There are times when we are dealt what we think is an unfair blow for making a mistake, but your mistake is well-understood, at least by me! I have given you a tough and undefined assignment. Under the circumstances, you are coping well, Son, even if you have some doubts."

"Dad, that's why I came to see you. I don't feel that I am coping well at all. A little guidance from you will be most welcome, as I have not yet gained a complete sense of just what it is that I am really supposed to be doing. I'm literally at sea and often frantic to get a clear mental image of where I'm going and what I should be doing. So many things are happening to us, some good and some bad... really bad. Our lives are upside down, literally. My eyes have been opened up wide, for I did not realize or even think that other civilizations could possibly be sharing our planet. It's been a real shock to my system, but in return, there have been some really nice occurrences as a result. Oh, there have been a few bad moments; I guess you have to take the bad with the good.

"I'm in somewhat disbelief that our brains are rapidly developing new skills, abilities, and thinking capabilities; it's utterly amazing. I'm confused, unsure of myself, feeling pressure to succeed, and at the same time, I am exuberant over the notion that we are breaking new ground and doing something that is useful and imperative to the survival of all and for the good of all.

"I'm sorry, Dad, for bleating on the way I just did, but I already feel so much better for it."

"It's understandable, Son. You have been carrying a heavy burden lately, and your direction has not always been clear to you. Keeping you in the dark a bit is perhaps beneficial, as you will clamor to seek more. Time and focus has a habit of cleansing the muddy waters that lie before you. Son, if life were simply following a straight line, what would you get out of it? Human beings are complex creatures, having an abundance of untapped skills and abilities. Following a straight line does not motivate the brain to think; it does not encourage the heart to have a conscience; it only serves to activate the primeval inherent traits of survival and basic needs to sustain life. A curve or perhaps a Mountain Ess has been thrown your way, and remarkably you are responding and responding well, even if you are a Doubting Thomas. What you can do today is significantly more than what you could do yesterday. Think what you will be able to accomplish tomorrow. Bravo! You must feel enriched in life, accomplishing what you have in such a short time span.

"I sense that you and Maggie need a little time together, not pursuing your assigned mission, but nurturing yourselves, doting on one another. Take a couple of days off. Go for a walk on the beach. Have a picnic, or go for a hike. Just selfishly share that precious time. Trust me: The path will become clearer once you give yourself a little free time to absorb the what is/isn't and the what isn't/is."

"Thanks, Dad. I know you're right. I have been so fully consumed I cannot distinguish the forest for the trees."

They rise from the bench, looking at one another, and then, Jake hugs his dad while a tiny tear creeps from the outer corner of his left eye. Their embrace is longer than it usually is, and anyone nearby can easily sense the deep emotions that exist. Jake waves goodbye and turns with renewed confidence, anxiously anticipating his return home. He walks into the kitchen and wraps his arms around Maggie, as if it has been a lifetime since he has done it.

"I love you, Babe." Tear stream from his eyes, and he is filled with heartfelt emotion. "You will never know how happy I am to be here with you."

They stand in an embrace for what seems an eternity, Maggie feeling so much relief that Jake has returned safely. She worried herself sick when she felt Jake's pain and knew something was amiss. When they finally brake from their embrace and lip-lock, Maggie asks Jake if he encountered any harmful or hurtful situations while away. Jake shows Maggie his right leg and Maggie cries out, "Holy shit, that's horrible looking. It's still bleeding. Jake I've got to get you up to the hospital. You need stitches."

While waiting in the emergency room for more than

six hours, Jake is fully knowledgeable and understanding of Maggie's dilemma about the events of this day and calmly says, "Sweetie, tomorrow how about we have a picnic on the beach?"

"Yes! Yes! Yes! Oh, Jake, I can't wait to be with you alone."

CHAPTER 18
Refresher

That morning, the November air was cool and burdened by heavy black clouds portraying threats of nothing but colossal doses of wet (west) coast rain. When it is dreary in November, you feel like pulling the covers over your face and going back into hibernation. It is quite a disappointment, since all the weather guessers have promised a bright, sunny day. Maggie and Jake were planning to spend the better part of the day on East Beach in Semiahmoo Bay, lavishing themselves with each other, sipping a little wine, and feasting on whatever delights that emerged from the fridge that morning.

"Maybe we should move to Plan B," Jake says. "Perhaps we could take a nice, easy walk up the Alouette River dyke or spend a day or two in Whistler doing what every other average person who goes up there does: eat, drink and shop. Oh, I forgot, most normal people go to Whistler to ski or sled or simply take in the natural outdoor wonders of the area."

Shopping— well there are lots of offerings if you are of the few who can afford, and of course, the usual "made in China" Canadian-type tourist trappings are ever so abundant, which they certainly don't relish.

A day in Whistler is quickly agreed up, and after a modest breakfast, Maggie and Jake are on their way. Katey stays home, which is all right with her, as she just wants to sleep off a cool, rainy, dreary day. Arrangements are confirmed with the boys to come over and tend to Katey's needs while Jake and Maggie are away.

Having to drive through Vancouver— in Jake's

opinion, the most car unfriendly city in the whole, wide world— is a painstakingly perfectly horrid experience. There is bumper to bumper traffic everywhere; construction occurs at virtually every corner; and stops of over three minutes are commonplace. Coughing and hacking over the smell of diesel fumes, wishing for ear plugs due to the intense noise, and having to put up with road rage antics of many makes Jake wonder why he ever suggested traveling to Whistler.

Once across yet another antiquated bridge— Lions Gate— and into West Vancouver, things begin to lighten up. The view along the upper level highway is simply stunning, overlooking the ocean, and they spy a number of awesome sites while looking over towards the Gulf Islands.

The narrow hilly mountain highway is somewhat risky to drive, given its history for accidents and mudslides. It's also fun to drive due to the curves, and one gets the real feeling that a racing driver might get during a tight race. Well, just north of Horseshoe Bay, Jake and Maggie are stopped by a mudslide. "Better days have been had," they comment; however, Jake and Maggie are after all together, and that is the most important thing. A couple hours later, they are once again on their way, hoping to get to Whistler safely.

Jake and Maggie are having a good time reminiscing about their past, playing Name That Tune, and singing along with oldies that are playing on the car's CD player. It is starting to lighten up for them, now having their minds fully focused on themselves; perhaps normal life is not that distant.

Jake, in a panic, slams on his brakes and pulls the vehicle off the highway, coming to an abrupt stop. A flock of whir-bits suddenly appeared in front of the car windshield and he interpreted their presence as an omen to stop. They witness a large cedar tree crash onto the highway a mere fifty feet in front of them, crushing a van load of would-be shoppers heading into Vancouver. They look at each other in horror and agree that the tree would have hit them had Jake not stopped.

"Jesus, what was that wave of black dots fluttering in front of the windshield before you panicked and stopped, Jake?"

"A flock of what I call whir-bits. I am convinced that they are non human aliens from some far-off place. Yesterday, when I was on that dry beach, a flock of the same eerie-looking birds directed me off the beach to a more inland point. I truly believe they saved me from the snapping turtles that appeared on the dry beach upon my departure. I have the belief that they are a good omen and that they are, for some reason, are acting like guardian angels. These creatures seem to share the same universe as those nine-foot freakin' two-headed monsters. It's a mystery where they came from and how they have now found our universe; however, I am glad they appeared when they did... You know, Maggie, maybe it's not that much of a mystery how they got here. They seem to exist in the same parallel as those freakin' nine-foot goliaths, and they found their way to our universe. Perhaps, I left death's door open. Maggie, this is the second incident on this trip; unpleasant things usually occur in three's, so I think we need to decide whether it best that we turn around and go somewhere else or carry on."

"Jake, we have paused now for about ten minutes. Wouldn't that pause disrupt or alter the natural sequence of events?"

"It certainly would place us at each point of progress at a different time... Yes, I do believe you're right, so it is likely okay to proceed."

Jake pulls their Mercedes coupe back onto the highway and, as looking into his rear view mirror, he sees rocks, trees, and other debris cascade down the hillside and cover the spot where they were parked. Jake puts the pedal to the metal in an attempt to put as much distance between themselves and the new slide behind them.

"Jesus Maggie, number three has just struck behind us."

"What?" Maggie replies, and then she looks into the car's right side-view mirror and becomes horrified.

The balance of the trip is uneventful, as they roll into the town of Whistler about at 1:00 P.M. Hungry by now, they decide to park wherever there is space— an interesting challenge— and walk into the center of town to find an appealing eatery.

The air is chilly, and every so often, a snow flake appears and melts on the sidewalk.

"We need to find a good restaurant soon, Jake, as I am really getting hungry."

"I am, too, Maggie, but so far, I haven't seen anything that is really appealing. I don't want one of those expensive restaurants, Maggie, that shortchange you on quantity. I need to find a good old American style restaurant that serves both quality and quantity."

"Ah, the Hard Rock Café is always a good choice, this I believe I have been looking for, do you agree, Maggie. Oh Yes, Jake."

While the café is teaming with eaters, Jake and Maggie are lucky to secure a table tucked into the corner away from the noisy hoards. Holding hands and stealing a few kisses make them feel like a couple of red hot, sizzling teenagers in young blossoming love. Distracted only by the waiter to take and serve their lunch order, they selfishly focus on themselves. Their eyes focus on one another in such a deep in a love trance that their sorbet melts in their spoons. Few prying eyes capture this romantic event, much to their delight, as it is so personal. It is truly their moment of reconnection.

Having now fully sated their appetite and confirmed their never-ending love for each other, they decide to rid themselves of this noisy eatery and overcrowded town center and hit the many hiking trails.

A good hiking trail with some meaningful challenge is good to revitalize one's heart and soul. Likely, it's better for the heart. Jake and Maggie are very quiet but assuredly close and warmed by each other's presence. They hike higher into the surrounding mountains.

November can be a bit of a shoulder season in the area when struggling to cope with the dying days of fall and the emergence of winter's presence. A little snow, a little rain, and a chilling breeze make you want to walk a little faster or secure a hotel room with a cozy fireplace. The thought of sitting in front of a fireplace with a bottle of wine, a few types of cheese, crackers, an apple, some red seedless grapes, and the love of your life seems more important than toughing out the dying daylight hours on an exposed rugged mountainside. Jake and Maggie both blurt out at the same time, "Let's get a hotel room with a natural gas fireplace and snuggle in!"

They check into the Fairmont Chateau Whistler Resort, and their room is elegantly decorated, complete with a natural gas fireplace strategically located for comfortable romantic viewing.

"Hey, Sweetie, it must be five o'clock somewhere. Let's get naked, open that bottle of fine white wine, and dine in front of this awesome gas-fired fireplace."

"Oh, I'm ready, Jake, oh so ready, but let's be close before we dine. I am so hungry to be with you, Jake."

"All right, Babe, I'm with you. How about a little white wine to warm the cockles of your heart, Sweetie?"

"Oh, yes. Any questions, Jake?"

"Just like old times."

Like mature adults in love with one another, they engage in such moving, tender, ever so stimulating love. Completely oblivious to the time and their surroundings, their devout focus on each other and their deep loving relationship brings them to the early hours of the evening. Feeling quite drained, they finally dine on more cheese, crackers, apples, and sweet red seedless grapes in the comfort of their own company and their cherished nakedness. It's perhaps a vulnerable position for some people, but it is oh so natural to them.

"Goodnight, Sweetheart, and thanks for such a wonderful day," Maggie says, in a loving tender voice.

"Goodnight, Sweetie, and thank you for being you and being with me today. I love you, Maggie."

"Love you, too, Jake."

In the morning Maggie, opens the curtains and receives a wonderful surprise: a brilliant sunny day in November. What are the odds of that happening around the west (wet) coast? Perhaps it's like winning big on the lotto— one in a million.

"Jake it's so beautiful outside. Let's have our breakfast and do a little hiking before heading home."

"I'm comfortable with that plan, Babe. Let's get moving before the day is gone."

Sticking to the lower trails, they soon start to turn their attention onto their mission in life.

"Jake, when you were off seeing your dad, I suddenly realized this mission was the most important thing that we could ever participate in, and I want you to know that I am ready to give it my all. I am so sorry that I didn't come with you to see your dad. I felt simply awful when you got hurt and I was not there to help you; I let you down, Jake."

"You didn't let me down, Maggie. I know that life recently has been a bit unbearable for you, and I understood your desire not to come with me. I really missed you, and now I am encouraged that we are now tight with this assignment. You really didn't let me down, Maggie, honestly... Let's head home now, Maggie. I am ready to see Katey, and I also look forward to planning our next move."

"I'm with you Jake. Let's go home."

Fortunately, a clear, bright, sun-filled, and glistening day brings with it a safer travels back home. The drive is actually nice and uneventful until they hit gridlock traffic in downtown Vancouver.

"It's good to be home again, Jake; I now feel that I can go on with our mission. Thanks for the grand time in Whistler.

"The pleasure was all mine, Maggie."

CHAPTER 19
A Genderless Civilization

"Good Morning, Sweetie," Jake says with real vibrancy and exuberance in his voice.

"Why are you so cheerful this morning, Darling?"

"I woke up this morning thinking about all the wild adventures our lives have taken in these past few weeks, and I also thought about some of our strange encounters and the wacky behaviors exhibited by our civilization. The world appears to be running off its rails with global warming, our excessive consumptive appetite, and corruptive human behavior."

"Wo, Wo, Wo, Jake, help me understand. What has any of this to do with you being so cheerful this morning?"

"Sorry, Babe, my mind is in overdrive, conjuring up exciting thoughts. I guess my comments don't connect or maybe all circuits were busy leading to my confused state of euphoria. I know we are on an important mission, and we have yet to succeed in understanding or comprehending who or what is responsible for the communication outages over Iran. In the night, I began developing strong urges to revisit Koidon in Naranna. It is important to strengthen our alliance with him and his people, as they have so many powers we simply don't have. We will likely need to draw upon their resources in the end to resolve this worldly event. It would be in their best interest to participate in resolving the issue peaceably rather than the world experiencing nuclear fallout and the like. A profound curiosity has developed within me to come to understand how Naranna has developed so successfully, and I must admit our own inability to determine gender is quite puzzling to say the least."

"So you have sex on the brain again, Jake!"

"Ha! Ha! Ha! Sexless I think, Maggie... Maggie, would you and Katey like to join me in a visit to Naranna today?"

"You bet, Jake. I can't wait."

Jake and Maggie quickly make and eat a hearty breakfast, clean up the kitchen, and attend to a few earthlike chores, like paying a few bills over the Internet and responding to the good e-mails and nuking the spam. Soon they are ready to make the journey. Jake collects his backpack and guns, and Maggie attends to ready Katey for her inaugural journey through a parallel universe.

"Jake, why do you need to take your guns today?"

"In case there is a navigational mishap and we end up in a not-so-desirable place."

"Thanks for your vote of confidence, Jake. Please leave your guns at home. Remember: I have fiery eyes!"

"Okay, Sweetie."

"Jake, I sure hope Katey is up to the journey. You know it takes a lot of energy out of us each time."

"I'm pretty sure she can make this one trip, Maggie. Are you ready, Maggie?"

Jake, Maggie, and Katey stand in the living room with both holding onto Katey's collar. Soon they disappear from the living room and reappear in the centrally located, park-like expanse in Naranna. Katey, is wide-eyed and whimpering a bit upon their arrival in Naranna. She leans hard into Jake's legs, nervously scanning the landscape. Katey soon begins to feel more comfortable in her new environment. Sniffing the ground beneath her feet seems to make her feel even more secure and comfortable.

There are many Exiztans carrying out a variety of activities in the park. Simple observation tells them that this is a highly family-oriented society, taking the time to nurture its offspring and evolve in its relationships. Playing what looks like games and having fun seems also to be a big part of their lives. Katey, Jake, and Maggie stand agape, sucking all this in.

Koidon, sensing their arrival, hastily makes his way toward them, not for fear that harm will befall his people, but because he himself is in joyful anticipation of seeing them again. Koidon is also looking forward to meeting Katey. Pets are not common in Naranna. As its civilization has advanced, the population seems to have abandoned comforts such as pets, as they, within their own society, have become more comfortable and self-assured. Peace within their inner selves, shared within their society as a whole, takes the place of attached comforts like pets. Intellectual comfort and stimulation is their inner peace.

Koidon extends one of his arms to greet Jake and Maggie. "It is a great pleasure having you return to Naranna," Koidon says with robust enthusiasm.

Maggie says, "A hand Koidon? Uh-uh. You can give me a hug. I am a hugger!"

Koidon smiles. He carefully and gently wraps his four arms around Maggie, giving her a little hug and a fish peck on the right and left cheek, European style.

"And this must be Katey. What a beautiful, simply gorgeous dog!"

Koidon very carefully extends one of his hands to shake Katey's paw. Katey seems somewhat uncomfortable at the sight of Koidon, but she nonetheless lifts her paw for a good welcoming shake after seeking reassurance from Jake."

"Come, I know Foinama is waiting impatiently for you. She has some herbalites[1] awaiting you."

Foinama is all smiles and gives Maggie a big hug and then turns to Jake and, without hesitation, gives him a big hug, too. Jake, feeling the warmth of Foinama, suddenly is no longer repulsed by her God-given appearance. He realizes that appearance is only skin deep; it's what's inside that counts. Foinama emits an aura of warmth and goodness that would convert the greatest

---

[1] Tea

104

skeptic in nano-seconds.

Katey is given a very warm hug by Foinama, and she offers Katey a neffum[2], which she holds in her left upper arm. Katey politely accepts the neffum and then gives Foinama that yearning look with a cocked head and wanting eyes, awaiting another treat. Foinama is delighted with Katey's response and immediately gives her another neffum.

There is much small talk around the table while they enjoy a hearty drink of gooseberry herbalite. Gaels of laughter emanated from their table as they re-acquaint themselves with each other.

Koidon suggests that Jake and Katey join him for a little fishing at the local lake. Jake thinks that that is a great idea, since he hasn't been fishing for many years, specifically since the the fees jacked up for a simple fishing license and that the fish stocks were nearly depleted.

Foinama suggests that Maggie might enjoy a visit to the center of town to do a little sight-seeing and perhaps enjoy a quaff at the local watering hole. Maggie thinks that touring the town is a terrific idea, especially the quaff part, and motions her acceptance. Maggie is pleased at the thought of having a less taxing day.

Koidon, Jake, and Katey prepare to visit Lake Myrah, a local lake five miles northeast of the town center. Fishing rods in hand, Koidon suggests that they hold Katey's collar, as they are about to experience levitation. Levitation is perhaps the most efficient and timely way to reach their local destination. Floating about one foot above the ground, they are whisked away. Although Jake has briefly experienced levitation while getting off the dried-up ocean bed, he and Katey experience light footedness, as their balance is at times in question. The feeling of air rushing past their body feels good and refreshing, similar to the feeling of riding a bicycle. Katey keeps looking up at Jake, seeking assurance that all is well. A very curious look

---

[2] Cookie

105

can be seen in Katey's eyes and the way in which she holds her head slightly cocked to the right. She is rightly proud to be in the company of her master and strange-looking, but nice host.

Koidon states, "Experiencing levitation is somewhat similar to riding a Segway. The more you experience the motion, the more comfortable you become, and once you are relaxed, your core strength takes over and provides you with comfortable balance."

Koidon is right, as usual. As they approach the magnificent emerald green Lake Myrah, both Jake and Katey look a lot more at home with levitation. Jake's face returns to its original color and Katey looks around in great anticipation that there will be a bevy of fresh scents upon their arrival.

Lake Myrah is dead-calm. A look into the lake provides them with a perfect reflection of themselves. Jake puts his hand into the water and approves of its warmth. This location has especially beautiful, colorful hillsides, as a variety of wild flowers spring up above the grass, highlighting their individual unique qualities and radiant beauty. Graceful-looking trees punctuate the landscape, gently swaying in the ever so gentle breeze.

There are many boats to choose, but none show any evidence of being equipped with a motor that burns fossil fuel. As a matter of fact, there is a great selection of rowboats, sailboats, canoes, kayaks, and a few slightly larger vessels similar to what human's refer to as "run-abouts". These boats all have small but powerful electric motors. Similar to Koidon's household appliances, when required, the motor simply draws its required power from the invisible electrical grid.

Having selected a boat, which would serve their modest needs, they power away from the pier for a short trip to Koidon's favorite fishing spot.

Katey always loves riding in a boat and is very comfortable with the warm air rushing past her. She loves to be with humans and just loves the experience of being included. Ideally, biding their time, waiting for the first fish to bite, Koidon inquires as to the current state of their infamous brain development.

"Koidon, Maggie, and I have been experiencing quite a number of interesting developments. To name a few, our eyes have become powerful telescopes; Maggie and I are now capable of releasing deadly laser rays from our eyes when our life is in peril; and we have learned to teleport ourselves around our own universe with pinpoint accuracy."

"I am impressed, Jake, but not surprised. You still have some major growth before you, and do not be afraid of the power that you develop. All talents, skills, and abilities that you and Maggie develop will be useful in your quest for the good of all."

"I am a little more than curious, Koidon. How do you know what is before us in our quest when we do not even know ourselves?"

"Jake, we have three hundred years of growth and development over you and your civilization; we know more than you will ever think. Jake, your travels through different parallel universes has indeed opened your eyes to the realization that other forms of life exist. Not all forms of life are friendly. Be very careful when crossing death's doorway, and never leave behind anything personal, as there are ways to be found?"

"Koidon, what do you mean by 'death's doorway'?"

"Jake whenever you enter another universe, there are two doorways. Be sure what is isn't, as it might mean the encounter of the Zingstones. The Zingstones are a lost civilization from our home planet, and they were very much about our civilization's development of body armor. A ruthless civilization they are, knowing nothing but death and destruction. We have had a few such encounters with them since living in Naranna. Do exercise a lot of caution, Jake, when entering unknown universes; I would be devastated if something unpleasant happened to you and Maggie.

"It is not I that should guide or steer you; it should be you in your rapid growth. I will assure you of one thing, Jake: My people and I will assist you if it becomes necessary to save this planet. We have an active interest in your success, as we share the same world, Earth. Remember: Your father is your guiding light."

"Koidon there is something that I have been meaning to ask you. It is rather personal, but I hope you will explain it to me."

"Now you're beating around the bush, Jake. I am not at all opposed to discussing any topic. As a matter of fact, we thrive on sharing information for the good of our race."

"Thank you for that, Koidon. I will be as succinct as a rambler like myself can be. On our first journey here, I couldn't help but notice— and Maggie did, too— that we were unable to distinguish a gender difference among you. To be specific, when I look at you and Foinama, there is no noticeable difference other than your facial differences. You don't wear clothes; your outer skin reveals what I think is the true you; and you all look the same, in terms of being equipped, if you catch my drift. This is truly puzzling to us, as we know that you are reproductive. You have children. We are aware that, in some cases, such as in the case of a worm, one can self propagate. We wonder if that is your situation. With our species men have penises and women have breasts and a vagina. The vagina receives the penis, and if all goes as planned, the women becomes pregnant, setting in motion the balance of the reproductive cycle."

Koidon develops a big, broad smile on his face and starts to audibly laugh. "Your observations are good, Jake. I like it. You're a thinker. There are many reasons why we display no visible evidence of difference, but I assure you there are differences. Our species has endured such warring atrocities over the centuries and suffered severe climatic shifts that our outer shell or skin has developed more like armor. This armor has been beneficial to us in fooling the

108

marauding night raiders and others who wish to delight in our females and devastate our families and our values. If, by observation, there is no difference, we believe this lessens the chance of our females being singled out. We will go to war with them as one unified force, and we have learned that this becomes an added strength, leading to our advantage. Females think and act somewhat differently, therefore confusing the attacker or attackers."

Koidon smile widens even further, and perhaps a hint of smugness appears as he carries on this conversation.

"Jake, be assured that we reproduce in a similar manner as your species reproduces. I am sure we garner similar gratification from the physical act, and yes, may I say it is simply and purely delightful. One huge difference exists with us: We are monogamous in our relationship, and we only participate in such pleasure when the female is ready to reproduce. Well that is not entirely true. We may endeavor in such activity on the odd other occasion, but again, when the female has such desires or we both concur. You earthlings— not all of you, but many— do not share this similar value. Jake, there is a strength that exists within our civilization: the fact we share an extremely close academic intelligent association with others. We all treat each other as equals and share an equal responsibility in the development of our families and our nation. We simply do not waste our precious time lusting over our next female conquest. That is not even a consideration here."

"Koidon, what you have just said is most amazing, but it seems odd to me to think that the female is in total control. I thought you just stated that males and females were treated as equals. Tell me how in the world can males and females be treated as equals when it is the female that is the dominant one and controls the when, where, why, and how many times, and so on? And just what is involved in preparing a female and, for that matter, a male for a 'love in' experience? Is it like experiencing a metamorphosis, dropping your armor?"

Koidon's broad smile on his face is now turning to a

sign of puzzlement.

"Wow, it looks like I just hit a nerve, Koidon. I'm sorry."

"Don't be sorry, Jake. Those are good thoughts that I have never questioned. First, the female control is a positive feature in our civilization, as it has reduced to the number of random, planned, and even opportunity attacks on our females to zero. Females are in control and are in control only within the context of them possessing the ability to reveal their genitals. Males cannot achieve this feat without causing the death of the female, so what would be the purpose? I suppose 'metamorphosis' is an appropriate term to describe the process of revealing the genitals, although I like to think of it as a heavenly miracle. The brain sends signals to certain parts of the female body, and within no time, the armor peels back, revealing the female parts. As this occurs, the male brain likewise sends signals, and the male reproductive organ emerges through the armor. A male's erection is only signaled by the actions of a female."

"Koidon, I can understand your lack of idolization of females. Basically, you are not faced with the visible differences that exist between man and women. This is a major difference between our species? Where I come from, too much idle time is generated by the male of the species seeking ways to get into the pants of a woman. It's like a game, and unfortunately, so many are obsessed with sex for the sake of sex. Young women in particular conduct themselves in such a manner that they leave themselves open to such seduction. Wearing short-short skirts and deep v-ed tops, and getting a bit tipsy on booze or drugs all result in sex at best... or rape or perhaps death at worst. As I see it, we dress for sex; we socialize for sex; and then sex dominates our society. Whatever happened to the moral code we once lived by and the good values society established? While sex and the obsession with it has always been within our society, it just appears to be going way over the top these days, and it is counter-productive to the

110

growth and development of our civilization. Sexual crimes and sexual predators are major contributors to the ruination of our society— not to mention greed. Demoralization of women and the fact that society establishes social inequalities between man and women appear to be all wrong. In some parts of our world, religion and government play a role in ensuring women do not share equal status in ruling and decision-making, and they also control their appearances in public. The creation, building, and proliferation of differences do nothing for the unification of the sexes, nor does it build esteem among women. Our species has a long row to hoe to reach a harmoniously balance. Thanks, Koidon, for a very frank and interesting discussion.

"Koidon, I hope you don't mind me asking more questions, but I am curious as to why you and your people have four arms."

"No, that's another good question, Jake. How much difficulty do you have in bringing in a big fish and getting it into the boat safely and unharmed, Jake?"

"Um! Well it is nearly impossible unless I can somehow manage to hold the line from slipping and then grab the net, oh, I have struggled with that before and you know what I usually do, I get help from someone else or risk losing the fish by jerking it into the boat unaided by net."

"Exactly my point, Jake! That is not an issue for me. See, I have a spare set of hands to make me more self-sufficient and efficient. Fishing is a good example, but let me tell you that having the extra appendages is most useful in almost everything I do. As we, as a species, were going through our physical challenges and changes to cope with our newly emerging and menacing environment, we developed in smarter ways than our prior selves. We began to realize the ultimate importance of the left and the right among other things, not only in the brain, but in the physical being. Producing four upper appendages eliminated the discrimination that would have otherwise existed between the physical left and right. So Jake, when I bring in a big fish, I hold the rod in my left hand, reel in with my right hand, grab the net with my other right hand, and sip herbalite tea in my other free left hand. A real multi-tasker I have become."

"I don't know just how many times I had wished to have just one other hand, but to have two would be the ultimate, as I am ambidextrous. I envy you, Koidon. Okay, Koidon, since you have so elegantly enlightened me with your last answer, perhaps you could explain why you have three forward facing eyes that I have come to understand. Why the one in the nape of your neck?"

"You're full of good questions Jake. I, like you, have two normal eyes, which give me good forward long and short focal view and left and right peripheral view. My third eye, located at the epic centre of my forehead, is my telescopic eye, which is so powerful that I can dial it in and see a maggot from a mile away. I recognize that you have developed telescopic vision within your left eye, which is acceptable for the environment you live in, but for us, it was important to maintain full normal vision in addition to on-demand telescopic vision. I use that as an example to illustrate the power and ultimate benefit that this eye provides when facing the enemy or discovering new environments."

Meanwhile, back in town, Foinama and Maggie have set out on their journey into experiencing the town center's offerings. Maggie is impressed with the overall cleanliness of the town. There is no garbage lying around, and everything appears to be placed with a specific purpose in mind. Wow, a civilization that cares about its surroundings and its environment. Truly amazing, Maggie thinks.

The first stop is an interesting aromatic herbalite shop. The air is full of wonderful aromas wafting from the shop and onto the street. These aromas lure them into the shop without hesitation. Once inside, they find that the walls are lined with a thousand varieties of herbalite. One small section of the shop is outfitted with bistro tables and chairs so that one can enjoy a cup and take a lead off one's feet. Freshly made berry cookies of many varieties are still warm and ready to for consumption.

Maggie suggests to Foinama, "A sample would be nice," and so they sit down, ready to be served. "Foinama, I want to treat you but if I don't have any money, how is it possible for me to do so?"

"Maggie, there is no need to concern yourself about that. We do things and obtain things more or less through a barter system and/or an information exchange system. This exchange here is recorded in a central computer system, and at some point in time, we settle up under either system. No one is too concerned about an immediate settlement, as it will even out in the end. All of the population is productive and giving here, and no one will ever do without there needs or wants being met. I must admit that our wants in a materialistic way are very low; therefore, our consumption is also low. We are real believers in accepting what nature provides, and as you have likely observed, nature provides an abundance of basic food needs, recreational needs, and sights. The environment is our number one concern, and we make sure it remains healthy."

Having enjoyed a cup of ginseng herbalite and an apple raspberry cookie, Maggie and Foinama continue their journey through the town. Maggie is surprised to see a lady's and men's clothing shop.

"Gosh, you don't wear clothes. How can a clothing shop expect to stay in business?"

Foinama smiles and says, "A vast portion of our population has integrated into your world, and they work and live in your universe even if it is only on a part-time basis. It is very important to us that we achieve this integration so that we may, in the future merge, our civilizations for the good of all. So, clothing stores are important to us and to our future, Maggie."

Wondering through the stores, Maggie notes that the clothing styles are very much of the current fashions in her world. This is not a real surprise, considering integration without detection is the motive.

They come upon a natural-looking water park right in the town center. Scores of Exiztans frolic in the water, swimming and diving off the low- and mid- height rock surfaces. It is great to see so many children out with their parents and the parents taking an active interest in the games and needs for their children's learning requirements. The beaches are spilling over with the local population, and a beehive of activity is occurring everywhere they look. Many of the Exiztans are playing net games similar to that of beach volleyball, although the ball is considerably larger and appears more sponge like. One thing is for sure: The population sure seems to enjoy the recreational side of life.

It is getting on to just before noon when Maggie first senses she is nearing a watering hole. The delicious smell of warm peach wine fills the air. There are other smells as well, such as that of dark ales, berry beers, and fruit ciders.

"Foinama, the smells in the air are luring me in this direction, and I so desire to acquaint myself with one of the local quaffs."

"I am also hungry," says Foinama, "what with all this walking and exercise we have had this morning. Just around the corner is the waterhole I mentioned to you earlier this morning, Maggie. I thought this might be a nice treat for you to have a new experience and have an opportunity to delight in healthy but delicious natural foods."

Maggie is about to order when the clerk states, "It's a great pleasure to serve you, and may I say it is great to have you visit our universe. You are the first of your species, to visit us in Naranna." He then states, "I work in San Diego on a part-time basis, working for a computer chip corporation. I am very familiar with your universe and enjoy my time there."

Maggie is taken aback by the fact that she is recognized and spoken to, as this really hasn't happened before in the usual social setting. She says that she is enjoying her visit here in Naranna and is looking forward to sampling a good wholesome natural lunch, not to mention the peach wine.

She orders a crock of warm peach wine. This is what lured her here in the first place, and for some unexplained reason, she needs to try something right off the wall from her former experience. Foinama orders the same stating, "Peach wine is an exceptional choice, Maggie, considering the food choices that they serve here. Peach wine compliments the natural food by providing the right mix of sweetness and flavor."

Over a delightful lunch, Maggie can not control her urge to ask Foinama a few personal questions.

"Foinama, I was hoping you wouldn't mind if I ask you a few personal questions, given the great differences that exist between you and me."

Foinama smiles and says, "I have no difficulty answering any question you have as it is our custom to share information for the benefit of our people and the survival of our civilization."

"Good, your willingness relieves me somewhat."

"It is our observation that you do not exhibit any sexual difference between yourself and Koidon, and we do not understand how an apparently genderless society can be so re-productive."

Foinama bursts out in uncontrollable laughter.

"I'm serious, Foinama, honestly. I see that you exist in what we would consider a family environment, living like humans do and making your lives very family-dominated. I am curious to understand the differences that exist between our two societies, as my observations thus far suggest you are a much happier lot living more serendipitously than we are?"

Foinama smiles and says, "Maggie we are a very happy and progressive society that values life foremost, and

Maggie, I want to apologize to you for my outburst. You just took me by complete surprise. We may appear to be genderless, but we are anything but, and life for us means the devotion to our mates and our family. Maggie, you need to know that our lives were not always this way. That truly developed once we settled into Naranna. Over the centuries, our physical form and appearance evolved due to warfare and climate changes. Females were once the target of many atrocities— rape, murder, discrimination, and slavery— at the hands of those from other civilizations. Earth's civilizations have experienced many similar atrocities, such as the events that have occurred in Rwanda and Uganda to name only a couple. For the survival of the female population, major evolutionary changes took place, which were not only for the betterment of the females but also for the entire society. Our focus became less sexual and more intellectual in nature, and our values and morals strengthened as a result of it. In our society females have full control over the reproduction of our species."

"You do?" Maggie blurts out. "In our society, some women sometimes exhibit control, but it is only in passive aggressive behavior designed to frustrate or punish men. You know, you give them the cold shoulder treatment, or they're cut off until you decide to let them in."

"Maggie, our control of reproduction is not to create frustration or punishment among the males; it is simply to protect the female population against predators. We are a society that involves males in every aspect of our lives, and that includes family growth and development. When a female knows that it is the time to bear another child, the actions of the female signal the male into action. When the female is ready— through a metamorphosis-type process— she starts to expose her genitals. The tough armor turns to soft, supple, pliable, silky, smooth skin and becomes ready to accept the male organ. As this occurs with the female, the male brain is triggered, and a similar process occurs allowing for the exposure of the male reproductive organ. This all occurs behind closed doors to preserve the sanctity

116

and purity of our love-making," Foinama states, emphatically. "Believe me: It is most pleasurable to get together in such a union, with the warmth of togetherness, the inner feelings that emerge from within, and the joy of what our actions bring to this world. It is truly wholesome and genuine, and it only strengthens our loving relationships and respect for each other."

"Wow," That explains our differences to a tee.That was intellectual enrichment for me."

"Come on Maggie there is more to see, and we don't have a lot of time before our mates and Katey return."

"You're right, Foinama. I really appreciate having this little discussion over lunch, and by the way, the quaff is simply to die for. Thanks for the experience."

Jake and Koidon are in deep conversation when Jake's fishing rod is nearly whipped out of his hand and the reel sings a familiar old tune of "zing".

"Holy catfish, Koidon! This must be a whopper. It's really fighting hard."

"Remember, Jake, we play catch-and-release here, so take your time and enjoy the thrill and challenge of the fight."

It is not unusual to latch into a thirty- or forty-pound trout in these waters. The population has agreed on a policy of catch-and-release, except for the occasional food source treat, thus giving the fish population a fair chance of maturing. The locals call this species of trout a flipper trout, as it often dances atop the water, supported by its powerful tail, and thrashes about, attempting to lose the hook.

"Wow," Jake says. "This is fantastic. I have forgotten how much fun it is to fight a fish, especially one of such size."

Jake's fight with the flipper trout lasts about forty-five minutes. Jake is exhausted, as is the trout. Koidon assists Jake in ensuring the successful release of the fish and its return to the lake unharmed.

"Oh, the fish will have a sore jaw for a week or so, and then it will be in the mood to be suckered again,"

Koidon happily laments. "That was a beautiful trophy fish, Jake. Just think how much bigger and stronger he will be during the next fight with a lucky fisherman. Maybe it will be me... Jake, time is marching on. I think we should head back to shore and then home. I sense, by the big broad smile on your face, you enjoyed the experience, Jake."

"I did indeed, Koidon. It was a thrill catching that fish; however, I want to re-affirm that I completely enjoyed our profound conversation. I have learned so much. Thank you, Koidon for a wonderful experience."

"My pleasure, Jake. And how about you, Katey? Did you enjoy yourself?"

Katey lifts her head off the boat's floor, looking at Koidon, and gives him a couple little woofs, acknowledging her pleasure.

Foinama and Maggie are wandering through an open-air market, where a few hundred vendors of all ages are attempting to lure the onlookers into the purchase of their wares. This is obviously a place that the local population really enjoys. Everyone wears a happy fish face. They are eagerly involved in the process of gentle, but not vulgar haggling for the best price, their arms holding cloth bags filled with their family needs. What an opportunity for a social exchange of trivia, a strengthening of relationships, and a thriving enjoyable experience.

Maggie says, "This type of sale event reminds me of home, but people aren't quite so spirited and happy!"

"I hear ya, but here, it is a real fun social event for us... Maggie, I think it is time to head back home now. I sense Koidon, Jake, and Katey are now on their way home."

Back at Koidon's home, there is an exchange of everyone's day's experience. The experiences and the awesome conversations held have made for a fun day and one of greater learning and understanding. There have been neither fighting hooligans nor wild unearthly-looking beasts. It's been just a downright wholesome "veg-out" day with great, friendly, unearthly-looking people.

Maggie and Jake realize that they have spent, again, more time than they originally planned, and indicate that they must return home and carry on with their mission in life, though they regret it. Rounds of thanks and hugs are made, and Jake, Maggie, and Katey soon re-appear in the living room of their South Surrey home, safe and sound.

Katey looks surprised, somewhat confused, but nonetheless happy to be home, and she goes straight into her bed in the family room, a safe haven for her.

CHAPTER 20
A Convenient Spin

The president enters the presidential briefing room, noticing the air has lifted somewhat, as there is some levity present. All those who are required to be there are accounted for.

"Gentlemen," the president says, "by the looks on your faces this morning, I figure you must have solved the world crises. The United Nations requests that we brief them on the communications black out over Iran soon. General, has the development of our response been roughed out?"

"General Whitmore, sir. We believe we have a very convincing spin implicating Iran and North Korea in a plot to construct an atomic bomb, with deadly intent to use it on Israel. Regarding the communications shield over Iran, we have yet to find a breakthrough. Major Pitt is here to fill you in on his thoughts on the spin."

"Go ahead, Major Pitt," the president states.

"Mr. President, sir, we are of the knowledge that Russia and Britain are also aware that General Lao of North Korea and his team of atomic scientists arrived in Iran about the same time as the communications shield appeared over Iran's air space. They have been most co-operative in assisting us in coming to a comprehensive understanding of such a liaison, and we are working collectively to gain a precise handle on their activities. Currently it has become nearly impossible to interpret those happenings, given the communications shield that currently exists. The President of Iran recently threatened Israel with his desire to blow Israel off the map. That comment was broadcast worldwide, so this would be no surprise to anyone and is an ideal link to the spin we have in mind. Iran has recently been boasting of their abilities in the nuclear field and they have expressed their desire in becoming a superpower threat to the world, or at least that is our interpretation. Sir, we believe we have the ability to use some facts and idle threats made public from Iran to convince the United Nations to consider sanctions."

"Major Pitt," the President states, "what you say makes sense, so lay out your perceived pitch to the U.N."

"Over the past few months, we, the United States of America, have been increasingly concerned with the activities taken by Iran in their development of atomic power and their public threats against Israel, not to mention those against the Western World. Requests thus far from the United States for United Nations to impose sanctions have not been supported and clearly denied. Over the past week we have developed even greater concerns that Iran is conspiring against the Western World and is developing atomic fusion for the specific intent to create an atomic bomb, not to just use their atomic knowledge for energy development. On the same evening that a communications black out occurred over Iran, North Korea's General Lao and his team of atomic scientists arrived in Iran. Ladies and gentlemen, this is not a sheer coincidence. This is an outright, blatant attempt on Iran's part to develop atomic weaponry and become a larger threat to the world than they are now. Iran has developed an impregnable communications shield to thwart our ability to monitor and assess these developments. This shield was deployed upon the arrival of General Lao and his team of atomic scientists.

"The world is at grave risk, and we demand that the United Nations immediately impose stiff sanctions if the following does not occur immediately: The communications shield must be dismantled, as it has disrupted worldwide commercial and military communication and worldwide security systems. An independent team of inspectors must be permitted to visit

121

and monitor atomic development with Iran's full cooperation. North Korea must also be inspected to ensure atomic development is not occurring. Both countries would be required to dismantle any of their atomic facility developments. Sanction requests are a worldwide boycott of their oil and rugs and worldwide trading suspension of all products, especially arms and uranium."

"I can work with that, Major Pitt. We will fatten it up some, and I will present this to the U.N. tomorrow afternoon. General Whitmore, an update on our Iranian mission would be appreciated."

"Yes, sir. We have finalized our plans of execution. We have broken into six teams, three members per team, and we have seconded six helicopters for the mission. Colonel Zorrograpidis and I will set up our command post in Kuwait. It is intended that we will commence our mission at 22:00 local time tomorrow, subject to your authorization. We will be outside of Iran's boarders by 05:00 hours the next morning, and I will be able to report our findings by 06:00 hours."

"Good Plan, General. It's a go for tomorrow," the president confirms.

CHAPTER 21
Oh Shit!

Jake and Maggie, while preparing to make a visit to a military headquarters in China, freeze. Out of nowhere, without prior warning, the house begins to shutter, shimmer, and shake. Suddenly, the air cools, and horripilation quickly begins dancing over their bodies to the tune of the blood curdling screams coming from the upstairs master bedroom. Katey begins barking with visible fright in her eyes, her fiery, red hair standing straight up on end, bristling as she nervously paces in fear. There is a huge crash of shattering glass that consumes the otherwise still air, and bedroom furniture is tossed and smashed, as if it were mere kindling wood.

Maggie quickly turns to Jake and screams, "Let's get the hell out of here and now! I don't know what is happening upstairs, but I know we are in peril."

"I'm right behind you, Babe."

Maggie flings open the doorway to the front hall only to discover the ugliest creature— surely not from this planet— staring her down and blocking their only logical means of escape. Due to the level of crime in the city, the gates to exit the back yard are all locked down, now preventing a speedy escape. Maggie screams and tries to return to the kitchen, when this six-armed, two-headed creature grabs her and throws her against the hall wall. Maggie hits the wall with such force that she breaks through the gypsum board and falls, limp laying unconscious on the tiled floor. With another arm, the creature hits Jake, and he is propelled through the living room window, landing against the rail of their veranda.

Maggie awakens to the thunderous sounds of the kitchen being torn apart when she hears the cries of Katey, as she is now being tormented. She, not knowing the whereabouts of Jake or whether he has survived the hallway incident, knows that she has to save Katey. Again, Katey cries out in pain. Maggie lifts herself up off the floor and stumbles into what remains of her once beautiful kitchen. Splatters of blood are readily evident on the walls, the floor, and even the ceiling. It's reminiscent of the helter-skelter slayings in California years ago. Katey lies silent on the floor near the fireplace, with her head lying in a small pool of warm, fresh blood.

Maggie screams and runs toward Katey when then creature suddenly re-enters the family room from outside and grabs Maggie once again, with the intent to rip her into minute shards of blood dripping flesh. Maggie, turning at once, shoots two blasts of white laser light from her eyes, hitting the creature in both of its heads. The creature reels, releases its intensive iron grip on Maggie, and then bellows an unearthly, deafening howl of ghastly agony. The creature staggers toward the double French doors in the family room and falls to its death on the patio. Its body starts to quiver. Then, cracks begin to develop throughout its body. Smoke emanates from the cracks, and soon the body simply disappears.

Maggie, not fully trusting the death of the creature, can't believe what has just happened. Once assured, she then turns her attention back to Katey, who is not moving, but she detects feint shallow breaths and a distant heartbeat.

Jake staggers into the kitchen, with blood streaming down his face and neck and onto his blood-soaked clothing. Maggie, realizing that Jake is hurt, runs to him and exclaims, "Jake, my darling, you're hurt! I am so relieved that you are alive! Let me look at your cuts to see if I can patch you up or if a trip to the emergency room is needed."

"I think I am okay. Just sore all over. My head broke through the window, and I body-slammed up against the veranda railing. Are you okay, Maggie?"

"Considering what I just went through, yes, I am okay, but I think I broke my pinkie finger. It is damn sore and a bit limp."

"Where is that bastard beast now, Maggie'?"

"I laser-eye-shot him, and he died outside. It was a gruesome death to be sure. His body simply cracked open, emitted smoke, and literally disappeared. Not a shred of evidence left behind. That is so strange, Jake. It is unbelievable to think that something so monstrous exists and can arbitrarily create so much chaos… Jake I am so worried about Katey. She is lying on the floor by the fireplace. She is breathing, but her breathing is shallow."

"Jesus, Maggie, I don't like the look of Katey. I think we better get her up to the vet and fast."

Jake scoops Katey up off the floor. Maggie grabs the car keys, and they are gone in a flash.

Anxiously awaiting the fate of Katey, Jake and Maggie start to recall the events leading up to this visit to the vet's office.

"Jesus, Jake, I still can't believe this has happened to us. Thank god we are alive, and I prey Katey survives. The house is in a total shambles. What a mess!"

"Maggie, it doesn't matter about the house. It is all fixable. The important thing is our health and that we are alive and able to tell the story. Considering the size and strength of that nine-foot ugly freaking creature, I am amazed we faired as well as we did. I am sure glad you have developed your laser eyes, or I doubt we would be here now."

"Jake, that creature's appearance is exactly like the one that I dreamed about. Do you remember my plight on the front street? And in the end, I laser-flashed the creature to death."

"Yes I do, and I still haven't replaced the ceiling fixture."

"This is all too creepy. I dream about this creature, and then, this creature enters our house and destroys it and maims us. I just don't understand how the creature got here."

"Maggie, it just occurred to me that our travels to parallel universes and your dreams might have triggered this event. Maybe we have left a door open somewhere or have left behind some evidence of our visitation."

"Do you really think so, Jake?"

"Yes. When visiting Koidon yesterday, he warned me to be careful that what is-isn't when crossing Zingstone's doorway, also known to the alien world as death's doorway."

"Mr. and Mrs. Bloomingdale, the vet is ready to speak with you," the pretty blonde receptionist says.

"Hold me, Jake; I'm not sure that I'm ready for this…"

"Hello, I'm Dr. Holdon. Katey has suffered a significant trauma. She has two broken ribs and is badly bruised throughout her body. She will be back to her near-normal self in a few weeks or so. I conducted a full set of blood tests on Katey, given her overall condition and age, and I am afraid I do not have very good news."

"What is it," Maggie states with alarm.

"Katey is a very sick girl. She is suffering from cancer of the liver and the cancer has spread into her right lung. I am sorry to advise that she only has a few months to live at best."

"Is there anything that can be done? An operation? Medication? Just anything?"

"Given the invasiveness of the cancer, I do not recommend putting her through chemo- therapy. It would not enhance life for her and would not likely extend her life either. Be kind to her. Don't let her become exhausted, and give her anything she wants. She will tell you in her own way when her time is up."

With the sad news, Jake, Maggie, and Katey leave the vet's office and return home. The silence is deafening, and Maggie silently weeps.

CHAPTER 22
A Plea

The President of the United States of America is invited to speak to the U.N. Assembly.

"Ladies and gentlemen, the gravity of my plea to you today must not be underscored. You have become aware that communications have been interrupted over Iran's air space, and I cannot overstress the damages this has caused to the worldwide security and surveillance system. We are now at a point of understanding the rationale behind the establishment of this communications shield and appeal to your good sense of judgment for the good of all. Iran has developed a very sophisticated communications shield that has blocked all out going communications and negated all surveillance and intelligence efforts. This communications shield represents a significant risk to the world at large and in particular to the Western World. Iran does not believe in the Western World's views and ideologies; it is clear by virtue of the messaging that has emanated publicly from Iran recently. Greater concerns rise from recent threats from Iran's president to the Western World and the ill will directed toward Israel. The evening the communications shield came into existence, General Lao of North Korea and his team of atomic scientists arrived in Iran at the specific invitation of Iran's president. It is no coincidence, I assure you, that this event and the communications shield deployment occurred simultaneously. Iran's president, over recent weeks, has been publicly threatening Israel with his intention or his hateful wish to blow it off this earth. He has also threatened the U.S.A. due to its war effort in

Afghanistan and Iraq. North Korea's president has also been badgering the world with its nuclear developments. It is clear to us that Iran and North Korea have agreed to a development pact to develop their joint capability in atomic fusion, and this represents a serious detriment to the world.

"Yes, the atomic bomb will soon be in the hands of very unstable countries, and if we do not collectively and aggressively move towards forcing there discontinuance of atomic developments, humankind and others will be at an unprecedented risk. We have grave concerns over the safety of the peoples of this world and specifically the peoples of the Western World, who share different morals, values, culture, and customs. The Western World has been in a constant state of challenge, which has been heightened in recent years by unprecedented and unacceptable attacks by hate-filled terrorists seeking to change the world, limit our freedoms, and force unwanted religious beliefs, habits, and culture onto us. We cannot and will not standby and allow any culture or society to impose their values, morals, customs, or culture on the Western World. We are prepared, however, and I repeat, we are prepared to live with other cultures and continue to adopt a level of respect, and I repeat, respect for the differences that exist. By not stopping Iran, North Korea, and any other country in the development of atomic capabilities, we place the world in serious jeopardy and at risk of major violent clashes. There is more than enough unrest and bloodshed in this world now, but atomic capabilities in the wrong hands will make the current atrocities look like *Alice in Wonderland*. The Western World has had a distinct advantage in protecting the world from catastrophic chaos in the past, because we have the technological advantage and we have agreements to not use this earth shattering technology against those who seriously oppose us. There is no certainty that situation would or will exist if atomic technology gets in the wrong hands."

"The immediate actions from the U.N. are needed more than ever in our history to prevent a worldwide holocaust. We seek the support of the U.N. and its membership in demanding that Iran and North Korea stop immediately their development in the atomic field of activity. We also demand that an independent team of inspectors be permitted to inspect the various facilities to determine and confirm the discontinuance of their atomic programs. We demand that Iran and North Korea fully cooperate and be overt with the team of inspectors. We demand that, if Iran and North Korea are not willing to discontinue their involvement in the development of atomic technology, then the U.N. will impose serious sanctions against those countries as follows:

"A worldwide trade embargo will be imposed on Iran and North Korea, with hefty penalties for anyone or any company exporting any goods or supplying goods to those countries. No exported goods from Iran and North Korea will be entertained by any country, including oil from Iran. All diplomatic relations shall cease between Iran and North Korea and the rest of the U.N. until preset conditions are met and maintained. I request the assembly honor our requests immediately so that all the peoples of this world may rest in peace."

"Thank you, Mr. President. The chair will now recognize our Iranian Diplomat to the U.N., Mr. Shaman."

"Ladies and gentlemen of the Assembly, we are simply stunned by the accusations forthcoming from the United States of America, but not surprised either. The U.S.A. is a bully in this world, imposing its views on all of us, as if for some reason they are the ruling class of Earth. They are not, and I repeat, they are not but simply one country with a world size ego. Iran is very interested in developing nuclear power for the sole purpose of generating electricity for domestic consumption. We are very concerned about the increased build-up of hydro-carbons and the damage that is being done to Earth, for which the Americas are mostly to blame. We view atomic energy as one good way to combat pollution and make life more pleasant and sustainable for our people. Iran has every right to further its developments in this field and should not be bullied and badgered by others. It is not our wish to bring harm to anyone or other nations, but we must prepare and secure ourselves for the future and not just rely on oil to fulfill our every need, given that oil is non-renewable.

"It is true that Iran invited General Lao and his team of atomic-minded scientists to work with Iran to further developments in the nuclear field. It is not true that Iran developed a sinister communications shield as purported by the United States of America. This shield is very much a surprise to Iran, and as a matter of fact, it is a detriment to Iran and our ability to communicate and to maintain our security surveillance within our own country. We want to rid ourselves of this life-threatening thing and demand that the U.N. force the U.S.A. to abandon their stranglehold on us. We believe that this shield is simply a sinister plot developed by the Americans in order to provoke our people and bring damaging sanctions upon us. We demand that the U.N. take appropriate action against the U.S.A. in demanding that they cease and desist in their sinister actions."

"As chairman of the U.N., I declare that it is now the moment that we must vote whether we agree with the U.S.A. in their assertions that Iran has developed and implemented a shield that prevents and interferes with global communications for the purpose of concealing its activities in the development of the atomic bomb. We must also consider Mr. Shaman's response to the U.S.A., the diplomatic representative of Iran's explanation that this is a sheer fabrication conjured up by the U.S.A."

The members of the United Nations vote down the U.S.A.'s proposal to apply worldwide sanctions on Iran at this time for its recent atomic activities, based on the lack of specific evidence brought forward.

CHAPTER 23
Secta-Iranian Mission

At precisely 22:00 hours, six helicopter gunships lift off from their designated departure points, each carrying three armed specialists and their equipment. Moving swiftly in silent mode, cruising about thirty feet above the land, they make their way unnoticed. Even if an odd farmer were to see or hear them, they would think little of it, as these scenes are replayed on a constant and continued basis by their own armed forces. An Iranian re-con is the most worrisome, but it's a risk they have to take. Flying at this low altitude is a difficult task for even the most experienced pilot, but it is a must to keep below the radar, even though they're assisted with night vision goggles and the most sophisticated radar and forward visual ground formation altimeters that depict unusual obstacles.

Communications are purposely scant from base to the pilots or from the pilots to their base; however, when needed, they use a special, random digital code that systematically scrambles the message during transmission and then unscrambles the coded message within the specially designed and secure headgear worn by the pilots and specialists.

Alpha Command sees their target approaching a few miles north of their current position. While it would be convenient to land the helicopter on the intended site, detection is not their intention. Given the noise that builds, especially during landing, running in silent mode means that they must land at least a mile from their target or risk discovery. A suitable landing site is chosen, and the helicopter soon contacts barren ground in a wake of its own dust storm. The specialists storm out of the helicopter, heading straight toward their target with purpose in their eyes and determination in their legs. The pilot must keep his machine running in the event that someone happens by to come or the authorities discover him. A risk of being heard is better than being trapped.

In no time, the specialists cut their way through the metal security fence and prepare to enter the facility buildings. An unusual number of security personnel are present at the gates and in and around the buildings. The routines of the security personnel are studied carefully and they, the specialists, find a hole in there pattern. Although chances are slim, it's worth taking the risk to penetrate the buildings.

The Bravo Command helicopter is in sight of their intended target and is now on its final approach. To their surprise, the building and surrounding lands are brightly lit. A beehive of activity is underway, which will present many challenges to the specialists. Having landed, they hotfoot their way to the designated target. About fifty feet from the rear, north-facing fence, the ground dips down, exposing what appears to an underground tunnel. This is a break they have not contemplated, and therefore, they need to pause to make a quick assessment. They collectively decide that this will at least be less risky, given the commotion observed on the site. Going in underground means confinement, but perhaps it betters their odds of infiltrating a more revealing part of the building.

Charlie Command catches sight of its target and now prepares for its much anticipated terra firma contact. The grounds are black, as if they were deserted. While some may be lured into thinking it's an easy target and want to rush right in, these knowledgeable, highly trained, and skilled men know that they cannot let their guard down for a second. What "is", is not necessarily the case. Getting themselves through the metal security fencing is done with the same level of care and skill as any other situation will prescribe.

Delta Command has the outermost distance to travel and must deal with very tumultuously jagged terrain. Their journey is harrowing at times, which makes the group of specialists suffer somewhat from nausea. The ground winds are now accelerating to ferocious velocity, creating eddies of dust and sand, which further impair their vision, bringing about an unacceptable magnitude of danger to their doorstep. The wind and unstable air mass condition increasingly deteriorates, forcing the pilot to turn around and initiate a return toward their home base. No one likes or wants to scrub a mission, but there are times when life over glory makes wholesome sense.

Echo Command is about halfway to their target destination when the helicopter develops engine problems. Attempting to smooth out the engine by leaning out the air-fuel mixture does not have any positive effect. In fact, the engine simply quits in mid-flight, forcing the pilot to auto-rotate to a safe landing site. Auto-rotation is a unique feature known to helicopters. The engine may quit, but that doesn't stop the rotors from spinning nor does it affect the controls that change the pitch of the rotors or affect the ability to descend or even lift the helicopter for a second for a more optimal landing.

Successfully down on the ground, the pilot, in all haste, removes the engine housing, seeking a fix. The sky is ebony black; the moon is full and vibrant; and the stars are shining brightly, giving the pilot some level of natural light to better observe the situation he is facing. After a few minutes of rooting for possible causes, he discovers the main fuel line is badly nicked and generous portions of fuel are leaking out of the line, starving the engine for fuel. Upon closer examination of the engine cover, he observes a bullet hole. At sometime during their flight, unaware of the danger that lurked, they took a sniper's bullet. This could mean that they and their flight path are compromised. With able-bodied help from the specialists, they make the necessary repairs with God's speed and are on their way with even greater determination than they had at the onset.

So far so good. If they have been compromised, a re-con team would have been on them by now. The Iranian's can scramble as well as any air force can. Feeling fortunate that the ground fire must have come from a rebel or farmer, they press on with renewed confidence.

Foxtrot Command perhaps has the most formidable and dangerous mission due to the populated areas it must travel through to reach its target site. Sticking to the fringe areas of small towns and villages presents them with more challenges than imagined. The outcroppings are numerous and larger than what was expected. Their journey is slow and interestingly harrowing, but the experienced pilot ensures a safe passage.

On the road ahead, they observe a convoy of military vehicles heading west. Fortunately, they are in a wide valley, but it is critical to take evasive action, so they cross the valley floor hip-hugging the eastern hill sides. Population density on both sides of the valley is about the same, so they take their chances and calculate the risks. One thing's for certain: Doing nothing will seal their fates.

Managing difficult flying maneuvers while still flying undetected through that situation brings about much relief, especially to the specialists. They want nothing more than to demonstrate their skills and be successful for the good of their country. To the seasoned pilot, it is all in a day's work. They all cheer when they catch sight of their planned target. The pilot slowly and skillfully brings his craft to the ground, keeping it partially hidden by a small ravine and some low growth scrub. The specialists scurry off and soon find themselves cutting their way through the metal security fence.

The Delta Command pilot reluctantly but knowingly grabs the mike and radios Secta-Iranian base in Kuwait.

"Delta Secta— Encountered severe ground turbulence, blinding sand storm. Mission scrubbed. Over. E.T.A. Base 01:00. Over!"

"Roger, Delta Secta. Thumbs up. Over."

134

The Alpha Command specialists seize the opportunity, knowing the gap in security will give them the time to cover the ground to the building marked "A" and slip into it via a small side doorway. Successfully reaching their target, they find the door locked but are not surprised. One specialist quickly pulls out his lock picking tools and, just in time, picks the lock and opens the door. Once inside, they observe about ten people tending to a massive garden of poppies. The entire building is a giant field of flowers, filled with its pure, sweet, and heavenly scent wafting heavily, awakening the senses within everyone.

Getting to the next building requires clockwork precision. Timing is critical. They have fifteen seconds to reach Building "B." Fortunately, the door is unlocked, and no one is in immediate sight. Regaining their focus, they stealthily make their way to the main operations area. More activity abounds. The building is full of processing and manufacturing equipment and automated conveyer belts connecting all the equipment. Small packages of white powder are coming off the assembly line and being driven by conveyer belts to the adjoining building. This is obviously an opium manufacturing plant, and it is currently in high production mode.

While they can assume the other building is simply a warehouse and shipping facility for the manufactured product— opium— they are thorough and quietly investigated to be sure. Feeling satisfied with what they find, and not wanting to increase their risk of detection, they make their way back to the awaiting helicopter.

When they are secured on board, the pilot slowly pulls up on the collective while increasing the engine revs. Safely in the air and heading back to their base, the pilot keys up the mike.

"Alpha Secta— Target is an opium growing, manufacturing, and distribution centre only. E.T.A. Base 03:00. Over".

"Roger, Alpha Secta. Thumbs up. Over."

The Bravo Company specialists quickly and quietly

135

slip into a dimly lit tunnel. They sense that the tunnel is deserted; however, with cautious optimism, they traverse through the winding damp, dank, and musty-smelling rat hole. After traveled about five hundred feet, they are startled by jovial voices erupting, melodiously snapping the tension in the air. With renewed caution, they hug the jagged, clammy, cold sidewalls of that ebon tunnel and creep cautiously, avoiding a menacing-looking family of teeth-bearing, humongous desert rats. Not a situation for the faint of heart. Soon they come into view of two burly security guards. They have been amusing that they would get through their evening of boredom by telling off-colored jokes and playing a game of cards.

The lead specialist picks up a good-sized stone and throws it past them, smashing it against the grating on the door that they were securing. The racket created by the rock thumping and scraping the metal jerks the guards into action. Rising quickly and spinning toward the noise, they open themselves up to their own capture. The specialists leap into action and capture their prey without any serious incident. Not wanting to kill them or otherwise bring about harm to them, they tie and gag them so that it would take an army of men to release them.

Grabbing the keys from one of the guards, they gain entry into a brightly lit hangar-type building. There appear to be hundreds of people harvesting a massive crop of marijuana. Keeping mostly out of sight, they observe nothing more than that single, focused activity: a grow-op.

Slipping out a side doorway, they soon gain entry to the adjacent building. Timing is everything in this business. Well, maybe sometimes its just plain good old luck. The guards are having a toke behind the building that the specialists have just entered, rather than circumnavigating the building.

As they creep through the western portion of the building, they observe huge, multi-tiered drying racks filled with freshly picked buds of marijuana. Progressing ever so

136

stealthily, they come upon the packaging and distribution portion of the facility. Few people are active here, as little product seems ready for the final processing and packaging. The specialists, donning powerful binocular goggles, do observe what simply blows their minds momentarily: The packaging labels contain these few words:

CONTENTS: GENUINE BC BUD

One cannot simply rely on the authenticity or quality of any product anymore, they think. Even the worldly criminal element uses deceptive tactics in the marketing of their inferior products. It's, all about the money, no shame, no honor: it's all business.

No time to waste. Detection comes with lolling, so no matter the distraction, they need to concentrate hard to back track their steps. As they step out of the building into the clear, warm air, an epidemic of confusion is cast over the facilities. The two guards have been found, and that has set off a mammoth hunt to locate their perpetrators. Knowing they cannot return the way that they came and seeing no one in the direction they want to go, they make a sprinter's dash for the security fence in a less brightly lit portion of an open field.

As they rapidly making their way through the security fence, their presence is detected. Half a dozen shots ring out, hitting one of the specialists, dropping him to the ground hard. His teammates, instantly engaging in rapid return fire, attempt to create a shield so that the downed soldier can be rescued. One soldier quickly grabs the downed soldier by the left upper arm, dragging him with sheer and utter determination and strength. The other soldier follows behind, shooting bursts of gun fire at the charging guards, inflicting some heavy damage and confusion on the pursers, sending a spine-tingling chill throughout the night air that would otherwise be serene and stagnant.

When they are safely tucked into the awaiting helicopter, the pilot quickly pulls up the collective, spinning the nose in the direction of their hotfooted pursuers and releases a heavy barrage of machine gun fire, cutting the remaining guards to ribbons.

The race is on to escape over the Iranian border. They know there was a pretty good chance that the Air Force would be alerted and scrambled for a serious game of hide-and-go-seek. Once safely away from harm's way, the pilot keys his mike

"Bravo Secta— Incurred hostile reunion. One officer wounded. Making direct return. Medics required. Investigated the facilities and determined marijuana grow-op processing, packaging, and distribution only, sir. E.T.A. Base 04:00. Over!"

"Roger, Bravo. Request acknowledged, thumbs up. Over!"

The Charlie Command specialists storm the darkened building, gaining access by picking the old rusted locks on the entry doors. Once inside, they think that no one has been in this building for quite some time, given the cobwebs and other litter and debris lying around. A peculiar hum is in the air, which captures their curiosity. Winding their way through, in and around deserted equipment and general waste, they come to a spot where the din level of the constant exasperating hum is magnified. Opening a much rusted and damaged steel door reveals a little-used staircase covered in heavy dust and debris and there further increase in the amplitude of the annoying hum.

Descending the staircase becomes increasing difficult, as some of the stair treads are either missing or more o less broken. Picking their way is ever so important to reduce the noise level and reduce the risk of detection. The noise is still building, thus they know that they are still heading in the right direction. What they don't know is what they are about to find or what danger lurks ahead for them.

At the bottom of the long dilapidated stairway, they come into a small, dingy, musty vestibule. Light can be seen under the doorway, so they know that they have stumbled onto something that is active. Their senses were heightened, as they know that the above-ground building now seems to have been nothing more than a disguise. They are about to get a firsthand look at what lies beyond the door.

One officer, putting his hand on the door, notices that it was about fifteen degrees warmer than the ambient temperature of the vestibule they are standing in. Placing one end of an electronic listening device on the door and the other end to his ear, he begins to carefully listen for what lies beyond. Deeming it safe to venture forth, he slowly turns the door handle and opens the squeaky door just enough for some visual observation. The hallway seems vacant, so they slide through and scurry toward the first open doorway that they come across. Once inside the room, they close the door to finalize their game plan for this underground search.

A moment later, they notice the answer on the wall before them. Unbeknownst to them, they have found their way to the visitor/worker briefing room. The wall holds the key to their findings. A gigantic schematic drawing of the entire facility basically unfolds before them. Studying the drawing, they determine that this is the active atomic development facility that the American authorities are convinced exists. While taking photographs of the entire facility schematics, it is revealed to them that the main access to this operation is gained some twenty miles south of their current position via an underground causeway.

The Iranian's have gone through a lot of trouble and expense to build this facility. Excitement bubbles like a silvery effervesce in their eyes over their discovery. Itching to see firsthand this complex development, they know a better opportunity will exist in the future. There is no way that the United States' satellite surveillance system could have ever picked up on this development.

They decide that they have enough information without going out looking for more or risking their operation's success. They hold the key in their cameras; they now need to secure that information and themselves.

Opening the door and ensuring that the way is clear, they rapidly make their way to the doorway leading to the vestibule at the bottom of the stairs. Climbing the stairs becomes tricky at best and then nearly impossible, as the wooden stairs literally disintegrate from under their feet. Making their way up the stair stringers is now a slow, daunting, and clumsy process; however, they endure without any major incident.

Getting back to the awaiting helicopter is easy, as no one is around guarding the abandoned, decrepit-looking facility. This vacancy has likely been created with intent and purpose so as not to draw any attention whatsoever.

The pilot quickly gets the helicopter into the air and sets his heading back to his base. Keying up his mike, he says, "Charlie Secta— Bingo. Above-ground building a facade. Secured photos of full schematic of underground atomic weaponry facility. E.T.A. 03:00. Over!"

"Roger, Charlie. Bingo bongo. Thumbs up. Over!"

Echo Command, somewhat overdue, comes into viewing range of its target. This target was once the site of an active research facility. While it has never really been confirmed, significant signs have led the weapons inspectors to believe it to be an atomic research facility.

Making contact with the ground, the specialists quickly and directly make their way to the security fence. Once having cut their way through it, they dash for the first of many buildings. On-site security is at a minimum this evening, giving the specialists a rather easy but cautious time getting through the facilities. A couple of buildings are completely full of short range missiles, rocket launchers, bazookas, automatic machine guns, land mines, and a menagerie of other weaponry.

Next they enter the largest building on the grounds, immediately eyeing the mass production of weapons of mass destruction. It is confirmed that this is a fully automated operation capable of producing thousand of various weapons, missiles, and bombs daily. Only a few people are on hand overseeing the automated mechanical operation, and they are all too busy to notice their infiltration.

Onward the team creeps to another building, which turns out to be the central shipping and receiving depot. There are a lot of security personnel hovering around the shipping bays, seeking out rebel thieves. It is apparent that this is a central source of supply for Iraq, Afghanistan, the Al Qaida terrorists, and a number of South America's rebel groups. Once inside, they are able to observe a number of shipments being put together, and they note the destination points. To their surprise, they notice one shipment of rocket launchers destined to Acme Building Supplies in New York City and another to Toronto, Canada, to the Iranian Muslim Adolescence Cultural Centre. The latter two shipments are items of interest and are immediately suspected to be for Al Qaida terrorist cells, which Homeland Security would deal with separately.

The Foxtrot Command specialists observe a strange stillness creeping into their minds, making the best of them feel the hair rising at the napes of their necks. Unable to identify what is behind this sense, they cautiously proceed beyond the security fence with the slyest of stealth and successfully reach the obscure side of a very large building. They have not been confronted by any security personnel, but the longer they are inside this compound, the more the specialists encounter symptoms of anxiety: hot flashes, like those that affect women who are going through and their change of life, and goose bumps rapidly overcoming them and seizing their bodies momentarily, and the sense that they are being stalked. The hair on the backs of their heads bristle, creating a feeling similar to the one you would get if a cougar or puma were poised to strike you from behind.

Into the dark building they creep, waiting, listening, their fears still heightening. Suddenly, the air becomes a wash of fluttering, as hundreds of vampire bats swoop down upon them, screeching. In a frenzied state, they whiz past their defenseless prey, ravenously biting them again and again, setting off motion detectors as they rise and swoop in a massive, dark, cloudlike formation. A bright flash streaks across the building, igniting it instantly, blowing it and its entire contents into minute shards of nothingness.

The Foxtrot Command pilot is stunned by hearing a mega explosion and bearing witness to a huge brilliant orange ball of fire rising one thousand feet into the air, expelling a mountain of burning embers and still afire pieces of building materials. Believing no one could have sustained life from that blast, he feels his team members are the unsuspecting target of a bloody booby trapped building. He immediately and without hesitation pulls hard on the collective and the helicopter is instantly airborne. Circling, what was once their target, taking one last look and seeing that all was still and there is no evidence of survivors, he sets a heading for his lonely and anxious return flight home.

That explosion has surely been monitored, and it will take no time for the Iranians to muster ground and air personnel to investigate and wipe out any remaining perpetrators.

The Foxtrot Command pilot keys up his mike.

"Foxtrot Secta— Specialists expired as a result of booby-trapped building. Massive explosion occurred. No hope for survivors. E.T.A. Base 03:30. Over."

"Roger, Foxtrot Secta. Ah shit. Keep safe. Thumbs up. Over!"

The return flight keeps the pilot on heightened alert, as he anticipates that at any moment he will observe on the radar some fast-moving traffic, but none comes into view. He witnesses no stirring on the ground and none in the air. It brings some relief, but he still stays alert and on guard.

A lot of distance needs to be traveled before jumping the Iranian border, and just about anything can happen. Murphy's Law usually applies especially during times of uncertainty, so why should he not be prepared? Never let your guard down.

The Bravo Command pilot picks up a fast approaching aircraft on his radar screen. Keying his mike, he says, "Bravo Secta— Re-con zeroing in. Breaking from flight plan."

The radio crackles with static and then blacks out.

General Whitmore and Colonel Zorrograpidis frantically attempt to make contact with the downed gunship, but to no avail. The radio is as still and black as a late night summer sky in Vermont, and it becomes blacker, acknowledging the ensuing onslaught.

Those left at the base, from where Bravo Command took off, begin getting sketchy but sad news. Stunning disbelief wafts among the soldiers, who believed that their plans were bulletproof in the making. What has gone so horribly wrong? This just can't be, think the men and women. Perhaps it is just a malfunction of their radios or an odd blip or skip in the area where they were traversing.

A Sergeant, sadly pacing the tarmac abruptly yells out to his mates with fright and panic in his trembling voice, "They're here! Look, there here!"

Sure as life itself, the four soldiers appear out of nowhere. One moment the tarmac is cold, dank, and lonely, and the next moment four soldiers are marching with victorious pride. Two of the soldiers are assisting the wounded soldier, and they are all wearing the proudest faces. There are ridged, and their heads are held high and proudly.

What a wonderful sight! They just stand in awe, watching their heroes marching with pride, beaming all over with knowledge they have made it through. Yes, they are heroes. They are home, and they have lived so that they can tell their strange survival story.

The men quickly regain themselves and scramble with cheers and joy to assist their buddies in their return. The medics are first on the scene, relieving the two soldiers of the glorious burden of carry their wounded mate. Upon immediate examination of the wounded soldier, it is determined that the wound, while serious, is not life-threatening. The returning soldiers are embraced by their buddies and shouldered like heroes, then transported to their awaiting ground transports. They whisk the wounded soldier off to the hospital and to the now awaiting medics.

General Whitmore is apprised of the strange return of the four soldiers from Bravo Command, and he immediately departs for their base, leaving behind Colonel Zorrograpidis to wrap up operations in Kuwait. During his return flight, General Whitmore begins recanting the recent events leading up to this incursion, and a broad smile grips his well-worn, haggard, and weary-looking face. Impulsively, he starts musing about the meeting in the presidential meeting room at the White House, during which a strange presence suddenly overtook the president, prompting him to stop the meeting. He hasn't given much thought to that event since that day, as life has become somewhat unbearable and ever so demanding, given emerging issues that need to be dealt with.

Now, giving that strange occasion full attention, he bears in mind that, while that paranormal event was fascinating, it was really a non-issue. No fear ever came over him. Only curiosity rose in his mind. The president was the only one who reacted with perhaps a tad of fear, but considering all that had been going on at that time, it was no wonder that he reacted the way that he did. Still it was an unexplained phenomenon. Fortunately, with no malicious intent, he wonders, with much conflicting skepticism, if this event is somehow connected to the safe return of the four soldiers this morning. Ah, it's pure crap to think about that as a real possibility, he thinks, and he simply dismisses the notion.

Arriving safely at the Bravo Base, General Whitmore quickly speeds off to the hospital, where the young wounded soldier is being cared for. The soldier is in the operating room upon his arrival. About to close him up, the surgeons notice the general and motion him to come in. The operation is completed with the use of a strong local freezing of the upper leg, so the soldier is conscience and aware of his environment.

"It's good to see you, son," the general states with heartfelt sincerity. "You are a hero to me, to your comrades, to your country, and, most importantly, to yourself. We are all proud of you and welcome back."

The general now turns his attention to the other reason for his trip here. He wants and needs to understand how these men were able to escape unharmed from a situation that would otherwise mean certain mortality.

"Son," the General says, "can you recall the events that led you and your comrades to appear on the base tarmac this morning."

With a big smile now overcoming his face, he responds, "Yes, sir, every last detail!"

"Please, share your experience with me," General Whitmore requests in a gentle but firm fatherly manner.

While the surgeon quickly stitches up the wound, the soldier takes in a deep breath of air and begins his dissertation of the facts and sequence of events.

"Sir, we were twenty minutes into our return flight when we noticed a fast-approaching aircraft on are radar screen. While we were taking evasive action, breaking away from our flight path in a steep climb to gain as much altitude as possible, a missile was fired from the aircraft, hitting us and blowing off the mast and rotor blades. It's difficult to understand, but miraculously, while the cabin did sustain significant damage, it somehow held together. We suddenly began a wild, uncontrolled, spiraling decent, and we all clearly knew we were about to meet our maker. Sir," the soldier stated, with tears streaming down his face, "my whole, albeit short life was flashing before me when total silence surrounded me. With my eyes now closed, the silence made for an eerie descent, but for some reason, it was not a horrible experience. If anything, I believe I felt that I was at peace. Then, unexpectedly, as if being scooped up by a big, white, billowy blanket, we were whisked from the cabin. It was a miracle, sir. We could feel warmth, perhaps like the warmth of being in a mother's womb, sensing a safe, caring, and nurturing environment. All the while, we were being jettisoned a lengthy distance and placed gingerly upon the ground. Where we were we could not discern. We looked at each other wondering, but we couldn't muster a word. There was no panic or fear in us; we somehow knew we were being taken care off in the present life or in our next. We, at that precise moment, were not at all sure. The 'white blanket-type presence' started to move back and forth, rising up, gently curling easterly, and then repeating the rhythm as if encouraging us to rise and march on. As we did, we instantly found ourselves marching to the music of 'God Bless America' with great stoic pride on the base tarmac, beaming with pride at our return and our anticipated reception. Those are the facts, sir. There is nothing more to tell. It remains a mystery what was behind our safe return."

General Whitmore stands and salutes the young soldier, thanking him for his succinct recollection of events. He has difficulty holding back tears of joy that he feels for the wounded soldier and his comrades. Placing his hand on the soldier's right shoulder and smiling, he pats him and then departs from the room and the hospital and returns to the base.

On the return trip to the base, he keeps mulling over the succinct words from the young soldier, shaking his head. Despite all the years that I have been in the military— and that's a lot— he thinks, I cannot fathom such an event. His story has to be a bunch of malarkey. What or who is he protecting? What really happened? He keeps thinking, and he quickly begins to develop a profound sense of disbelief. Suddenly remembering that Bravo Command found a marijuana grow-op, he begins developing a plausible theory of events: They co-opted with the Iranians to smuggle out marijuana and faked an encounter with a re-con and the subsequent crash. They were then intercepted by ground transport that delivered them to the airport or within reasonable proximity. This seems most probable to him, and besides, the soldiers wound is not life-threatening, thus it could have been staged or self-inflicted.

Now back on the base, General Whitmore summons Major Hoolihan. He instructs the major to quietly investigate the runway beyond the visual sight where the four soldiers were first spotted. He is in need of any evidence identifying suspicious activity— tire marks or tracks in the surrounding area, any evidence of the helicopter. The major is clued in on the general's suspicions and knows the expectations of the assignment. Major Hoolihan, while obeying orders, feels distraught, having to do what she is about to do thinking that those men— her friends, her comrades— are under that level of suspicion. Why? It is so like military to think that a distinguished general cannot buy into the supernatural even for one moment.

General Whitmore summons Captain Bronson to his temporary office, which is somewhat unbefitting of a now five star general.

"Captain Bronson, sir!" he says, saluting the General until his acknowledgment lowers his arm.

"Welcome back, son. We are so relieved to learn of your return. You are a hero tonight, a brave soldier."

The General isn't quite as robust in acknowledging this soldier's achievement as he was with acknowledging that of the wounded soldier. His suspicion is running fairly high, although he does not want to exhibit any sense of suspicion or indifference. But, his difficulty is intensifying.

"Son, I know that you just went through a harrowing experience, but would you please tell me, in your own words, just what happened and how you managed to get back to the base."

"Sir, shortly into our return flight, I noticed a fast-approaching aircraft on my radar screen. Breaking away from our flight plan, I induced a painfully steep climb, twisting and contorting our tense bodies, gaining as much altitude as could be mustered from that old gunship. A menacing missile was fired from the incoming re-con, shattering our future. We lost our rotor blades, but luckily the cabin held together. We suddenly began a swift, rappelling, uncontrollable descent, and for certain, I felt death was imminent. I was scared, sir, scared that I would not see my family and friend, that this was the end. Unexpectedly, by what I don't know, we were taken from the cabin. It was a miracle, sir. I sensed I had entered a safe, environment. Then we seemed to be just gently placed on the ground. I had no idea where I was. We just sat there, looking at each other in total utter disbelief. The next thing that I remember was marching to the tune of 'God Bless America' with great pride on the base tarmac, beaming gloriously and celebrating our return and sensing a much anticipated reception. Those are the facts, sir. There is nothing more to tell. I am in much shock in understanding this event, as I am sure you are in somewhat disbelief."

"Are you sure there is nothing more you have to say, captain?" General Whitmore firmly states.

"Yes, sir," Captain Bronson states. "That is exactly what happened, nothing more and nothing less. I swear, sir."

General Whitmore probes, "Bronson, doesn't it strike you as a bit odd that an air-to-air missile fired from the re-con didn't evaporate you and your gun ship?"

"Sir, I would like to think it was a miracle performed by our maker and not something odd. It simply wasn't our time to leave this world. I have been thinking about that indirect hit we took, and I have determined that my quick and gut-wrenching, full G-Force evasion tactic is what saved us and kept the cabin basically intact, sir."

Hmm, thinks General Whitmore, I suppose that may be a possibility, I need to mull that theory over a bit. "That's all, Captain Bronson. Thanks for your verbal report. Send in Lieutenant Paycheck, Captain."

"Ye, sir."

The stories told by Lieutenant Paycheck and Lieutenant Cash, the other two specialists on that ill-fated gunship are identical in terms of the description and sequence of events that took place. Each man has his own way of expressing himself, his experiences, his fears, anguish, and, in some cases, his own doubt about what that billowy white blanket really was; however, in essence, the messaging is the same.

General Whitmore is in a quandary, not fully believing the soldiers' story, coping with the supernatural and his own beliefs. He feels he can't face the president with any sense of sanity indicating that a ghost or some supernatural presence suddenly appeared and saved the soldiers' lives.

He now turns his attention to Major Hoolihan, hoping that she will uncover the plot that is so fixed in his mind. Waiting causes his stomach to rumble and to seize up, sending tremors throughout his troubled and aging body.

Major Hoolihan appears in General Whitmore's temporary office only to find the general clutching his stomach and reeling with acute pain.

"General Whitmore, sir, do you need a medic?"

"No, Major, I think my peptic ulcer is just acting up again. Aging is a painful process. Thanks, Major, for your concern, and by the way, don't ever get old, and that's an order... Major, what information do you bring regarding your investigation assignment?"

"Sir, I have combed every square inch of area in and around the western end of the runway and I found nothing: no evidence of the helicopter, no evidence of vehicle tracks. Nothing looked out of place. On my return back to the most western edge of the runway, I did notice something odd and out of place. About ten feet from the beginning of the tarmac, I observed three and one half sets of footprints plus one drag mark, which I could determine came from a wounded soldier. These footprints and drag mark in the sand led me to the edge of the tarmac and then only small trace evidence appeared, as the remaining sand from their shoes was consumed. Sir, what was strange to me was the fact that before seeing the first footprints, I observed that there was nothing. It looked like they were just placed in that location and they began their journey home. What might be a scarier thought, sir, is the fact that they may have re-entered our universe from another parallel universe?"

"That would be conjecture, Major. I am only interested in facts" the General blurts out. "That's it, Major? You have nothing else to report?""

"That's it, General. There is nothing else to report."

"Major Hoolihan, you're dismissed."

General Whitmore is visibly upset but isn't quite sure which bothers him the most, the peptic ulcer or the fact he might have to take the butt end for what now appears to be a plausible happening. Embarrassing and belittling at his age, he could do without it.

The Echo Command specialists, now quite satisfied that they had uncovered a munitions factory, only retrace their steps out of the facility. They encounter no resistance and are quite relieved as they return to their awaiting helicopter. The pilot coolly and collectively increases the engine revs and slowly pulls up on the collective, achieving an airborne status. Setting a heading toward base, he settles in for the long ride and hopefully uneventful ride home. He pilot keys up his mike.

"Echo Secta— Located munitions factory. Over. E.T.A. Base 04:00 hours.

"Roger, Echo Secta. Fly safely. Thumbs up. Over."

The Foxtrot Command pilot, Captain Wily Nelson, carefully navigates his way back toward base, skillfully negotiating his way around the jagged hillsides and other obstacles. Alone in his gunship, his mind keeps drifting back to the scene of that blown out target, his buddies who have fallen. He begins to shake uncontrollably, and sweat pours from every pore in his body. He knows he will meet his fate if he doesn't get his act together, as there is no room for error flying at this low altitude. He finds himself breaking out in song "You're always on my mind" and becomes more relaxed and focused.

Approximately three miles from his point of exit of Iran, he comes under a barrage of ground fire. Without thinking, he pulls up on the collective and makes that old gunship dance as if it were precariously balancing on the head of a pin. Twisting turning and contorting that ship in hopes of avoiding any significant damage, he takes flak through the cabin and the side window. Pressing on toward his destination with sheer determination, he takes another few hits, this time causing damage to the engine. Now flying with diminished engine performance and some difficulties maintaining overall control of the gunship, the Foxtrot Command pilot keys up his mike.

"Foxtrot Secta— Mayday! Mayday! Mayday! Location one mile from scheduled exit point out of Iran. Gunship hit, going down. Iranian dogs will be on my butt. Request ground support. Over."

"Roger Foxtrot— Request granted. Land safely. Thumbs up. Over."

Unable to maintain sufficient air speed to continue flying, the pilot, sets his gunship rather hard on terra firma, causing the right side carriage support to collapse, thus snapping off the rotor blades and bringing the gunship to silence. Once the dust settles, Captain Nelson grabs his automatic AK-47 rifle and scrambles toward the border. The dogs are not far behind, and Captain Nelson is hoping the wreckage of his gunship will afford him a needed few extra minutes of distance.

The Iranian dogs, in hot pursuit, soon come upon the wrecked gunship and discovered that the pilot has fled. Again, they race away like a pack of starving wolves seeking to ravage their prey. Like the energy and enthusiasm of a rekindled fire, the adrenaline is boiling over and the scent of their prey lingers heavily in the air.

An Iranian gunship appears over the horizon, with its floodlight illuminating the hillside. Captain Nelson ducks for cover just in time to evade detection. Imminent danger now gone for the moment, Captain Nelson again races up the hillside, gasping for breath. Legs aching and heart pounding, he crests the hillside. He is now in sight of the Iranian border, but there is still a daunting distance to cover, with the dogs on his backside, a gunship somewhere overhead, and less ground cover screening his progress.

Captain Nelson thinks, I ain't submitting to those bastards, come hell or high water; I'm getting across that border, and he pushes his short legs beyond what is possible to close that gap between his location and the Iranian border.

The Iranian gunship bursts over the hillside, lights blazing again, illuminating Captain Nelson, as if he were a go-go dancer on a brightly lit table of attraction in an over-packed house of sleaze. In an alternating zigzag pattern, Captain Nelson runs, dodging the ground strafing emanating from the bloody beastly looking gunship. Running for his life, knowing that he cannot out run that gunship, he turns and fires a burst of rounds from his AK-47, and the gunship explodes in mid-air, hit by a ground-to-air rocket launched by his awaiting team at the border.

Captain Nelson could kiss the ground at this moment, but the thought of those Iranian dogs hot on his tail drives him into another race for his life. The Iranian soldiers, having now spotted Captain Nelson, begin firing at him. Again in an irregular zigzag run, he fearfully races toward his awaiting team.

The Foxtrot ground crew spots Captain Nelson nearing their position. Also knowing that he is in hot pursuit, they cross the border with guns blazing and intercept Captain Nelson. Racing back to the border, they come under continual fire, but that are spared the rod, so to speak, and now head safely back to their base.

CHAPTER 24
Unexpected Terror

"Good morning, Sweetie. I have read some interesting articles in the newspaper this morning."

"What's up Jake?"

"The President of the United States of America made a passionate plea to the United Nations yesterday, requesting that sanctions be imposed on Iran due to its continued development of the atomic bomb. This activity has been accelerated by a joint development with North Korea. This is strange, as it seems the United Nations voted that plea down due to a lack of specific proof that Iran is engaged in such activities. Apparently Mr. Shaman, Iran's representative to the U.N. denounced the U.S.A. for spreading lies, and he accused the U.S.A. of blocking communications over Iran and now demands the removal of the communications block. Given what we know, it doesn't make any sense that the U.N. would vote down this plea, unless the members are in dire need of oil or they are in the back pocket of Iran.

"Well, that might be a bit of an overstatement, but it is pretty obvious the U.N. is not necessarily on the Western World's side of things. That's probably a bit harsh as well but nonetheless strange.

"They have procrastinated in the past, and all hell had broken loose. Remember Rwanda and Uganda?"

"That's just terrible, Jake, but you have to remember the U.N. members do not have access to the information that we do, and besides, they are merely humans."

"We really need to work hard to resolve this

communications block and in a hurry, before it is too late to reverse the damage that is being caused. It appears that the U.N. is useless in resolving the mighty and powerful issues facing the world, but they are pretty good at getting the majority to support native rights throughout the world and resolving other issues of lesser conscience."

"Uh, uh, uh! Jake, let's not get to that level of criticism, as it is counterproductive. We have bigger fish to fry. Do you have a game plan is mind, Jake?"

"I'm still mulling one over in my mind, Sweetie. I think we need to go snoop around in China. It's interesting that China recently placed its space program under the direction of General Xaing, a five star general, perhaps a brigadier general, who now presides over China's Air Force, Navy, and Army and— guess what— it's aero space programs. Whenever the military becomes involved in things, there are no guarantees the world rules will be honored. We think, by what we saw, that the Russians are buffaloed at the appearance of the communications blockage over Iran. So, that perhaps makes China our next suspected target."

"Jake, before you think about leaving on this wild goose chase, will you please tell me where exactly you want to go in China. Remember that it is my navigational skills that get us there safely."

"I will give you plenty of notice; trust me. But for the moment, I am still mulling over the possibilities. I think I received another hint from Dad this morning."

"What was that Jake?"

"I was looking at the atlas, and I thought that Guiyang in southern China was the secret site for space military weaponry development and space operations. I was about to suggest to you that this be the target location when I had an urge to look at the Atlas again. I then realized that Guiyang is the center of the joint space operations working in co-operation with Russia, Britain, France, and the U.S.A. This couldn't be the location of a covert space operation, as each country has their staff there working in conjunction with all parties, thus ensuring the ethical practices and space developments that have been agreed to. It therefore means that any secret covert space operations have to be centered elsewhere. For some reason my eyes focused on Nenjiang, a few hundred miles north of Beijing and close to the Khingan mountain range."

"What's so special about Nenjiang?"

"It makes perfect sense, given Nenjiang's location. The mountainous region makes it easy to hide the activity and develop underground bunkers, silos, labs, monitoring stations, and the like. The location would also make for a perfect launching point if you had an intention of invading North Korea or Japan. Taiwan is a bit more distant, but it is doable. If China were interested in expanding its presence— and there have been many subtle hints that they are— those three countries would be in harm's way. Tibet— well, that maybe a stretch; however, given the number of patriates living there, it would only take a nudge for China to seize fuller and undisputed control and rid itself of Tibetian dissidents much to the chagrin of the Dalai Lama.

"Maggie it's only a hunch, but I think China is up to something big. China is a hugely populated country that is under pressure from its people for the better life. If you consider that China has a population base of over 1,200,000,000 people and probably another 100,000,000 expatriates, they can quite conceivably consider taking over the world. China's population continues to spiral upward, and its population is becoming more difficult to control. They are slowly learning that they have to be more lenient and giving to their population. Simply suppressing the people no longer works. The fact that their expatriates know there is a much brighter world outside of China and its clutching controls is a testament to that theory. They have the freedom to develop themselves for their best interests without restriction on family size, and they have the freedom to be truly entrepreneurial."

"Those are some good points, Jake, especially the

octopus network of immigration around the world. The expatriates maybe the key to China' success in taking over the world, thus helping them become the masters of the new world order."

"Yes, Maggie, those are my thoughts exactly. Maggie, the way that I see it, China is in a good position, given its controlled population and its force of expatriates should they be promised wealth and power outside of what is currently known as China. The expatriates can take over high ranking positions around the globe, if the right conditions exist, and become China's eyes, ears, and enforcers... Okay Maggie, I am ready to venture forth to China and see what we can uncover."

"Where is it exactly that you want to go, Jake?"

"Sorry, Maggie. Could you can put us three miles due north of the city limits of Nenjiang. It's not likely going to put us exactly where we want to go, but at least we won't have to traverse that distance by shank's mare. I don't think Nenjiang is a likely tourist destination, so we would likely stand out. The less distance we have to travel overland, the better."

"Okay, Jake, I will get us there; trust me."

Jake and Maggie stand in their living room and prepare for their journey to northern China. As they hold hands and both think hard of their intended destination, they soon disappear from their living room and appear within their extended telescopic eye-sight outside of a massive military base in northern China.

"Jesus, Maggie, you're right on today."

"It helps when you are precise about where you want to go, Jake."

"This is not going to be easy. I have never seen such fortification surrounding any facility before, and, Christ, look at the number of heavily armed security personnel. They are everywhere."

"Jake, from our vantage point here, we have the benefit of the visual of this base, at least what is on the surface. Perhaps it would be beneficial if we were to

156

mentally map out the base and attempt to find a rationale for its layout, identifying key points on the base."

"That makes a lot of sense, and this action may save us time in the future."

For the next hour, Jake and Maggie painstakingly map out the base. They come to realize that this is not just an Army base, like they thought it might be, but it is also home to the Navy, Air Force and a special anti-terrorist unit. Given the combination of armed forces collected on this base, it is apparent that this is a major operating headquarters.

From their vantage point, there is no visible evidence that a space program is being operated, which means that the facility is underground if it exists at all.

While comparing their mental notes about the base, they are surprisingly confronted by a small group of base armed security personnel.

With rifles menacingly pointed at them, they are commanded to about face and place their hands behind their backs. Having their hands shackled, they are roughly handled and led off to an awaiting truck and transported into the nearby military base.

It is eerily uncomfortable having the soldiers solemnly and placidly staring them down. No one says a word during the short ride to the base; however, Jake and Maggie suddenly discover that they can communicate with each other via mental telepathy. In a short space of time, they agree to be mum about their real reason for being there and devise a quick tourist excuse. They also agree that they will take whatever might be dished out and that they will maintain a constant state of communication. When they feel safe or are left alone, they will devise an escape.

Jake and Maggie are quickly separated and taken to independent holding cells. Jake is shoved into a small cell and suckered punched in the stomach a couple of times. Having slumped to the floor, he is then left alone and locked in the cell.

Maggie is taken to a similar cell and is sexually

fondled prior to being beaten about the head. She, too, is locked in the cell and left in a nearly unconscious state.

The next morning, before the sun rises above the horizon, Jake is abruptly yanked from his cell and brought to a brightly lit interrogation room. Jake's surroundings can only be described as nothing more than a medieval torture chamber, complete with a stretching rack, ball stretcher and squeezer, nipple puller, and a freshly bloodied guillotine.

Strapped in a chair, Jake is affronted by two burly, wrestler-type officers of the Red Army and is savagely beaten without cause. At least at that moment, Jake cannot understand the beating. No words are uttered. Jake's tormentor quizzes Jake as to where he entered China and the purpose of the intrusion.

Jake, still reeling from his beating, states that he entered at Beijing Airport, all the while spitting fresh blood from his mouth.

"You lying bastard! Where did you enter China?"

Before Jake can respond he is hit hard from behind, and then, he takes a right hook in the mouth. Jake slumps into unconsciousness, still strapped to the chair.

When Jake wakes, he knows that they are seriously getting into his head space. He suddenly realizes that he is no longer sitting in a chair. He is lying down, butt naked, on a stretching rack. A large bucket is suspended over Jake's chest, and it is dripping a single drop of cold, icy water every other second. This is Chinese torture; it plays on the mind until you go insane. Jesus Christ, I need to get out of here, Jake thinks.

"Welcome back to your reality," states one of the Red Army soldiers. "Where and how did you enter China?"

"I told you I arrived on Air Canada, flight 169, Vancouver to Beijing."

"Where is your airline ticket stub? "

"It was in my pocket the last that I looked.

The soldier yells, "Liar! You don't have a ticket. You didn't fly into Beijing Airport. Security at Beijing Airport has no record of your entry into this country. You have no immigration stamp on your passport. You are a spy… perhaps?" Demandingly, he insists, "One more time: where did you enter China and why?"

Silence. Jake communicates with Maggie and discovers that they have abandoned her in the cell with no food or water. Jake feels relieved that they have not injured her further. They feel that things are not going to get better and that they will seek a split universe as a safe haven. Maggie indicates that she would do most of the thinking due to Jake's precarious situation and that she will attempt to catch Jake in her flight to a safe split universe. Jake agrees that, no matter what is befalling him, he will not lose communication links with Maggie

"Speak up, asshole. I can't hear you. Perhaps a little stretch will improve your memory, you son of a bitch."

Ng, the officer in charge, flips a switch, turning on the stretching rack. Jake can hear the gears engaging while gnashing to correct there alignment. Pain from being stretched begins to emerge, and he feels like he is being wrenched by a vice. The pain intensifies as his legs and arms are stretched beyond what he once thought his muscles were capable of. Now Jake begins to scream as intense pain spreads throughout his entire body. The machine stops its advance, but it doesn't let go either. Jake's pain threshold is not high at best. He holds his breath for fear that, if he has to breathe again, he will simply break in half. The pressure he is enduring is so intense, and the constant drip of water on his chest is nearly driving him insane, when…

"Tomorrow a little pressure on your balls might improve your memory," Ng says with a sneer… "Think very carefully, asshole. We look forward to our meeting tomorrow." The sneering smile on Ng's face grows with the pleasure of anticipating the pain that he will inflict upon Jake tomorrow.

Jake is crudely dragged back to his cell by the scruff of his neck without abuse; however, the continued sneer on the officer's faces is enough to turn a roaring lion into a wimpy pussy cat.

Jake immediately communicates with Maggie through mental telepathy and alerts her of the fact that he is now alone in his cell. Very sore and tired, but otherwise all right, Jake knows that this may be their only opportunity to escape. He is most interested in seizing this opportunity, considering the alternative that he will face tomorrow. Both Jake and Maggie think hard about a split universe within the base compound, and in a matter of seconds, they are again together. They have a good cry and hug each other as if they can't remember when it was that they have had their last hug? Jake has a great deal of difficulty maintaining his balance while standing or walking, as every joint seems to be pulled apart and not as capable of supporting his frame as it once was. Maggie puts her arm around Jake and helps him move onward.

This place is mind boggling; the reality of the vastness of the base is more than a bit scary. They feel very relieved that they can wander, with however much difficulty, somewhat openly, as they doubt infrared scanners are operational in the open areas of the military compound. All the while that they are exploring this vast facility, they keep one eye on the lookout for trouble. The base is heavily populated with sailors, infantry men, Air Force personnel, a lot of heavily decorated brass, and administrative staff.

At least at this point in time, they find no evidence of a space operation. If space operations are located here, as they suspect, they guess that they have to be underground. But where?

They are about to pass by a military police officer and his guard dog, when the dog starts to act strangely, sniffing at Jake's leg, then growling confusedly and pulling at his master's leash. The officer turns to see what the commotion is all about, then shrugs and commands the dog to heal. Moments later sirens begin to blare and words are communicated over the radio speakers. Jake and Maggie turn to each other saying, "I guess they have discovered that we are missing." Maggie suggests that they lay low for a time, as foot traffic is building and they seem intent on re-locating them.

"Jesus, Jake, that cop and his nosy dog are coming back."

They quickly leave the street and enter a modest building, but the dog can obviously maintain and follow their scent as the cop follows behind. The gap is closing, as the cop knows he is hot on their trail, but he appears somewhat miffed at not being able to see them. The dog is pulling hard, wanting his handler to speed up, but he can't as he is running flat out. Jake and Maggie spot a high-lift crane starting to lift its load. They scramble, hell bent. Jake can hardly tolerate the pain, but he knows he must to be able to jump onto the lift. Where they are being taken is anyone's guess. They don't care. They just know that they have to put some scentless space between them and the dog, and for the moment, they are out of harm's way, as the entire base is out hunting them down. A few questions remain in their minds regarding the dog and its handler. They know their last known location. Will they latch onto the fact that they have escaped via the crane lift? So far, it appears that way. Or, will they be smart enough to think that they appear in a separate universe, thus promoting the use of infrared cameras?

Over the next half-hour or so, a number of military and non-military personnel come and leave through the interesting set of vaulted doors across from where Jake and Maggie are hiding out. The guards appear to know who is entering and therefore seem quite bored with the ensuing events.

They think that they will follow an individual or group of individuals that enter the guarded vault-type door; however, they have to be right on their heels, as there is little time during which the door remains open. A risk of detection exists, but that excites them. The unknown always pumps them up, makes them pant, and makes the heart flutter. Oh the adrenaline rush...

Just as they are about to make their move, there is a huge commotion, with troops running and chanting, "Death to Canadians. Death to Canadians." They remain still and silent a let the soldiers pass. It is obvious that they are in a panic to locate Jake and Maggie.

General Xaing is personally interrogating the prison officers about the escape of his special prisoners. The fear, desperation, and rage that exist on Xaing's face speak volumes about the magnitude of the Canadians' escape. Colonel Ng is withstanding a harsh dressing-down for his failure when General Xaing suddenly, without further provocation or hesitation, withdraws his 9-millimeter and shoots Ng between the eyes. Instantly dead, he slumps to the floor, expelling volumes of blood now pooling around his limp, lifeless, mutilated head. General Xaing, not missing a beat, orders the other prison guard to remove and dispose of Ng's body. Quickly, the body is removed and thrown into a freshly dug trench, then the assisting prison guard is shot for his incompetence and thrown in the same trench, then buried. General Xaing paces back and forth, seething and reeling. He snorts to his most senior attending officer, ordering the immediate capture of the Canadian spies.

"I don't care what it takes. Find then. Bring them to me dead or alive. It's your call. Dare not fail! We cannot risk the secrecy of our operation. It's my ass that's on the line. You can bet your ass will be on the line, too."

"Maggie, I don't know what has come over me, but I need to get home and get home now. I'm feeling nauseous. Perhaps something has ruptured in my stomach.

"It's okay, Jake. Things are too damn hot for us here anyway. Let's get home and tend to your needs.

They hold hands and focus their minds on home, and soon they appear in their own living room, all right but a little less for wear.

CHAPTER 25
Home Again

"Hi, Katey. It sure looks like you are glad to see us? What are you bringing us, a squirrel? Ah, you are so sweet. Jesus it feels good to be home again, Sweetie, but I wish I felt better, given these friggin' injuries."

"You know, I think that I have the perfect remedy for you."

"What's that, Maggie?"

"How about I pour you a stiff shot of single malt scotch in a heated brandy snifter, and I think I will pour myself a not so stiff shot of Martell V.S.O.P. Medallion "Old Fine Cognac" just to be different."

"Wow, you sure know how to please, Babe. It has been a rough couple of days. I am feeling a little better now; however, my stomach is very sore from the abuse I took. After all I am, not very experienced at being a punching bag."

"Perhaps a good night sleep will improve things, Darling."

The next morning, they are late to rise; however, they both are feeling better and anxious to resume their mission in life.

"Jake, there is something wrong with Katie. Look."

Katie has almost instantly developed a large sore on her right shoulder, and it has just burst open. Puss oozes from the wound, and small, white, wormlike fatty tissue emanates from the wound. The more they wipe the wound clean, the more puss and fatty tissue appear.

"Jake we have to get her to the vet now. The poor girl is really suffering."

They bandage her up the best that they can under the circumstances and take Katey for what will be her last ride. She is a strong-willed and determined dog. She walks to the truck, hops in, and walks herself into the vet clinic. You can tell that it is painful, but she still has her dignity and pride. They will miss the old girl, but she is now free to take on her next assignment and make others very happy. She has surely made the Bloomingdale's very happy during her short ten-year life.

It is a sad day for Jake and Maggie. Silence is deafening on their return trip home, although it is evident they both are weeping. Jake feels like he has just had is guts ripped out again, and Maggie feels the same way. Neither one can focus, as the loss of Katey overwhelms them so. One down day to honor and celebrate her life is warranted.

CHAPTER 26
The Eagle's Nest

Major Hall and his team of experts have spent many sleepless nights working overtime to crack the mystery surrounding the communications shield that is suspended over Iran. They have conducted a series of tests on their satellites and their own systems and nothing seems askew. It is a living nightmare not to be able to figure out this very complex situation.

National security is in jeopardy; his military masters and the president are getting impatient, with no evident progress being made. What makes matters worse is the fact that no feedback of any kind is being received by the worldwide security operatives. Most unusual, he thinks, although he is experiencing a similar vacuum within his closely linked global network.

This is truly a black day for the president, as his credibility, and the credibility of the nation, is coming under question. The U.N. is demanding action in the removal of the communications shield over Iran and the Democrats are demanding to be informed of the issues facing the country. Other world leaders are beginning to question the United States' ability to maintain its once proud record of world security. The global media continues, unabated, in its search for a story. Relentless in their worldwide probing and snooping, they have netted nothing.

"Major Hall," yells Captain Willis, "we have reason to believe the two rogue satellites have been activated, sir."

"Captain, what's happening?"

"Sir, we have noticed that the primary heat shield

165

has shifted it position ten percent east. We think the satellites are preparing themselves for an orbit change. This is odd. Since we detected their presence, they have appeared dormant. We are keeping a close eye on them and will monitor any activity."

"Well, Captain Willis, that is good news, even though we, as of yet, don't know what they are up to."

Major Hall calls Colonel Britch.

"Sir, a positive development has occurred with the two mysterious satellites. We now believe they are active, and perhaps they are being prepared for re-orbit."

"Keep me up to date, Major, and thank you."

Captain Willis starts to observe other movements on the satellites, and they are starting to maneuver further away from Earth. While not moving very fast, in the last hour, they have moved five hundred miles further into space. There is no change in the condition over Iran; the shield is still firmly in place. The team is still highly suspicious that the two rouge satellites have everything to do with the communications shield; however, they have not figured out how.

Captain Willis searches the world over to pick up a transmitting link to the two satellites, but to no avail. That is odd, he thinks, as they are always able to intercept the transmitting signals and listen in. This isn't so in this case. Does it mean that its operation is robotic or preprogrammed, or is it a communication source beyond human conception?

A flurry of activity emanates from within as they test and examine every possibility related to the movement of the two satellites. A tense aura overcomes the Eagle's Nest, as all present are totally absorbed in their work. Not knowing the meaning behind the sudden activation of the two rouge satellites is raising suspicions that national security is about to be even more seriously breached.

Major Hall begins debriefing Colonel Britch. The colonel's face shows grave concern, and as he paces the floor, he knows that it is time to brief General Whitmore.

His dilemma is that there is no sufficient information known to determine when and how the United States' security will be breached, but he knows that this time the jig is up.

"In all my years in military intelligence," Colonel Britch states with angst, "I have never encountered anything quite so bizarre. We can't just sit and wait for all hell to break loose; the lives of Americans are at stake. What the hell is going on?" he muses in disgust. "I'll be speaking to General Whitmore now. If the situation changes at all keep me posted."

"Yes, sir," replies Major Hall.

Major Hall screams, "Captain Willis, Alpha 14 is starting to send a distorted signal over China. Sir, the monitor screen has now blackened out. No, that can't be. Oh God."

Major Hall stands in front of Alpha 14's monitoring screen, frozen in time, shocked at what he has just witnessed. The Eagle's Nest is immediately put on red alert.

The communication's block is still in place over Iran, and now it also covers China. Only time will tell if Alpha 13 and 15 will also experience a black out once over China. Eyes are closely monitoring those screens. A hush comes over the Eagle's Nest as Alpha 15 nears China. Its monitor begins to develop wavy lines, which in time turn white as snow, and it, too, blacks out.

Major Hall, Captain Willis speaks out, "We have now lost all communications with the *USS Omaha*. Sir, it is currently anchored off Taipei."

Colonel Britch is again briefed, as it is obvious that whatever has happened over Iran has also clouded China. Colonel Britch alerts General Whitmore of the developing situation, and General Whitmore immediately confers with the president.

CHAPTER 27
Panic

One would that the world has just blown up based on the unusual level of activity taking place at the White House. Aides are scurrying hither and yon in the hallways and in and out of offices, as if they were hungry mice looking frantically for cheese. Panic embraces their faces, and inner mayhem appears on the horizon, given the look of the frustrated fatigued interns. What you know you can understand. What you don't know is simply another matter that brings about confusion, impatience, and fear. It can be simply described as an over-active beehive under the direct siege of a hungry bear determined to feast on honey. Phones are ringing off the wall; fax machines are smoking-busy with non-stop messaging; and the secured military Internet lines are running slowly, given the humongous volume of traffic.

Air Force One is reported to be landing at Andrews Air Force Base in Virginia, bringing the president back to Washington from an all too short vacation at his Southwest Texas Ranch. The president's chopper is standing ready amid a heavy fortress of well-armed special military units to rush the president back to the White House. Military brass have all been summoned and are amassing at the White House. The CIA, NSA, FBI and others are lockstep behind.

The Pentagon is abuzz with activity, hundreds of cars filing in and filling the parking lots and the underground. Nary a word has been uttered, just a lot of comings and goings.

The media, such as they are, have caught wind that

something is up, and there just might be a bonus for a catchy headline and cover story. They are jammed at the front gates of the White House, demanding to know what is going on, but they are bluntly ignored.

The Chief Director for the NSA pulls up to the White House but is whisked through the underground parking lot and away from the prying media, giving no one a hint of what crisis is looming. And a crisis it must be to gather the Joint Chiefs of Staff and anyone with power for what appears to be a national or perhaps a worldwide crisis.

There is much speculation among the media about possible Muslim extremists blowing up some nightclub or, even worse, flying another plane into some important building, maiming and killing hundreds of innocent people. How about that crazy leader of Iran? Maybe he actually has got an atomic bomb and is threatening the U.S.A. to back off of Iraq and Afghanistan. Maybe its China invading Taiwan, or maybe it has to do with North Korea's dictator, who can finally threaten the world with his new toy, the atomic bomb. One thing's for sure: It is big.

Air Force Chopper One arrives at the White House in its usual blistery dust storm. Before the president can exit the chopper, the surrounding grounds fill with heavily armed Navy Seals, an elite force within the U.S. Navy. The president is completely shielded from view and is escorted to the briefing room.

"Gentlemen," the president says, "I am stunned at the absolute silence you have demonstrated here. As your president and commanding officer you are expected, damn it, to keep me apprised on a minute-to-minute basis as to what is happening. Just what the hell is going on, a palace coup or what?"

General Whitmore pipes up, "Mr. President, with all due respect, given what we think is going on, we are not sure enough that our own lines of communications are fully secured. We cannot risk or permit the enemy to hear our conversations or let them believe retaliatory measures are being contemplated."

"Well," the president says rather indulgently, "apprise me now in the comfort of our secrecy."

"Mr. President, a few hours ago, the Eagle's Nest reported an activation of the two rogue satellites. It appears that they are being repositioned another five hundred miles further out in space. At this time, we are not sure of the purpose of the repositioning, nor do we know who or what country is behind this action. Only an hour ago, we lost communications with China, North and South Korea, Taiwan, and Japan. A black hole exists there, and Iran is still black. We have also lost all communication with the USS *Omaha*, one of our aircraft carriers under the command of the Seventh Fleet Pacific Command. All verbal and visual communication tracks have disappeared. Mr. President, these satellites monitor air and ground movement between the forty-fourth parallel and the Tropic of Cancer around the globe. We are currently totally shut out of knowledge in this area. The CIA reports central Asian operatives have gone cold, and they have been doing everything in their power to raise anyone, but as of a few minutes ago, to no avail."

"General," the president quips, "this can be no less than war. Who is the enemy anyway?"

"We don't know, sir. We are totally in the dark? Our closest operative is Mr. Lee in Bangkok. We have alerted him of the situation and have dispatched him to China to report back his finding. We do not expect to hear from Mr. Lee for two days, given the communications black out." General Whitmore further states, "Global Proctor's Bureau Chief reports that it believes they witnessed the possible launch of seven or eight ballistic long missiles in the northern China region. Global Protector unfortunately cannot make a confirmed sighting, as this event began to unfold when our communications links became distorted and blacked out. Russia has confirmed that many of their communications satellites are giving distorted imaginary, confirming that they too are in the dark with respect to that part of the world. We, as of yet, have had no feedback from China, but that is to be understood, given the cloud over that entire area."

"General Whitmore," the president states, "we do not know the status of the USS *Omaha*? There are seventeen hundred odd men and women aboard that craft. It is imperative that we know whether or not it is subject to any form of attack. I want two stealth bombers dispatched to fly over Taipei and report back their observations.

"Gentlemen," the president says, "given the fact that Global Protector believed it witnessed the launching of seven or eight ballistic missiles, I think we should move some atomic subs from the Seventh Fleet into waters far enough off of China's coast to avoid detection. What are your views Gentlemen?"

Admiral R.J. Ewing interjected that he has already alerted the captains of the two atomic subs currently based off the Marshall Islands to prepare for war maneuvers off the east China coast. "Deep-penetrating warheads are being activated as we speak. They are currently on orange alert. We also think it advisable to move some of the larger vessels of the Seventh Fleet toward China. We need to be careful not to alert suspicion, and therefore we will proceed slowly."

"Execute the commands, Admiral," the president replies.

"Yes, sir."

"Damn. What really is going on?" the president orally reflects. "We need to speak to the Chinese Ambassador and in person. If war is being waged, diplomacy dictates we are entitled to be informed before aggression is asserted. There must be some logical explanation to what's happening. We at least might gain some intelligence through a carefully crafted discussion. Loni, the President's personal and confidential secretary, I want to speak to the Chinese Ambassador to the U.S."

"Yes, sir, right away."

"Gentlemen, we are now on Red Alert. You must be accessible twenty-four hours a day and avail yourselves within one hour of my calling."

Around the table, each member swears his allegiance to their country and utters his acknowledgement and commitment to be available upon demand. General Whitmore is responsible for briefing the president, and the others are required to update General Whitmore of any change or information breakthrough.

"General Whitmore", the president presses, "what are the results of our covert mission in Iran".

"Mr. President, the good news is that we did discover a very sophisticated underground atomic development centre in a very isolated part of Iran. We have the full schematic drawings of the facility, which we intend to prepare for you and brief you on for a showdown with the U.N. We also identified a weapons munitions factory, which is supplying Al Qaida, South American rebels as well as other worldwide terrorist groups with light ground missiles and armaments. A major grow-op of marijuana was discovered as well as an opium manufacturing depot. Sir, the Iranians are dirty up to their ears, and we have the proof that we were looking for.

"The bad news, sir, is that we lost three of our specialists from the Foxtrot Company. Those brave men fell prey to a booby-trapped abandoned facility. They did not have a chance, sir. The Foxtrot pilot, Captain Wily Nelson, encountered a harrowing return, losing his gunship to enemy fire. He escaped with a little assistance from his ground support team, who made an unauthorized breach of the Iranian border.

"On another note, Bravo Company encountered an enemy re-con, and their gunship was destroyed. It is still a mystery how the pilot and crew were unharmed in the incident, and their evacuation of the gunship is still under investigation."

The President interjects, "What is the essence of the investigation, General?"

"Sir, there are some unusual circumstances surrounding the return of the Bravo Company to base that make is difficult at best to determine authenticity of events."

"Cut the double-speak, General. What is it that you are trying to say?"

"Sir, it appears that a paranormal experience occurred that we have been unable to verify."

A chuckle erupts among the sitting members, which makes the general squirm in his seat. The president, with a smile on his face, challenges the general to be more specific, since he confesses mind reading is not his forte.

"Sir, at my expense of being thought less of— something strictly military— while it is not yet fully explained, these men appear to have been lifted out of their seriously disabled gunship and deposited unharmed at the edge of the base runway. We have not located the gunship and believe it is somewhere in Iran, and our investigation suggests nothing out of the ordinary other then they appear to have been placed where they emerged."

"That's good, General. Well, keep me informed if anything changes with that situation," the president states with a little smirk on his face.

"Yes, sir."

CHAPTER 28
Golden Key

"Good morning, Sweetie, are you game for a little romp in the hay?"

"Um, it's too early. Give me time to wake up."

"Okay, Babe, but given my age, when the urge is here, don't delay to long. You snooze, you lose."

"Oh, Jake, I love you."

The next half-hour brings about a bushel of happy returns, which can only be shared in their own special way. What a great way to wake up! Usually they think, if they wake up, it is a blessing, but this is sheer blissfulness, an added bonus to the day.

After some freshly brewed Kona coffee, toast, and some stimulating reading from the daily newspaper and great conversations about worldly events and other lesser topics, Jake thinks it's time to return to China.

"Oh, Jake, I'm not sure I can bear the pain. Remember our last experience?"

"Last night, when you fell asleep in your chair, I tuned into a confidential conversation at the White House."

"How the hell did you do that?"

"Oh, I just focused my attention on the White House, and I started to hear a very interesting conversation in my head. The United States is preparing to go to war against China. The U.S. believes China is somehow behind the communications interference over much of Asia, and Global Protector thinks it witnessed the deployment of several missiles, although they were not able to confirm it, as the lights went out, so to speak. Sweetie, this is serious stuff. We need to close the chapter, even if we risk serious harm. I would like to get back to that split universe that we were in just prior to our quick departure home. Is it possible to just arrive there, or do we have to do this in two stages?"

"Leave it with me, Jake. I will do my best to get us where you want to go."

Jake grabs his packsack, guns, and ammunition in preparation for their return visit to China. Forget the Passports; they will just get us killed quicker if we are caught, he thinks. Maggie has no objection to Jake's action, considering their last welcoming in China, and she makes sure that Jake has her .22 semi-automatic and several spare loaded magazines.

As usual, with a hard thought of their destination, a few minutes later, they appear in front of the vault-type door. Even though they have traveled this way a number of times, they are still awed by the ease and safety with which they can travel. Why would you ever consider public transportation of any sort when all you have to do is stand in a room and think hard about your arrival at your requested destination?

After waiting a couple of minutes, a couple of administrative-types signal their intent to enter through the vaulted door. Maggie and Jake slip in behind them in lock-step and gain passage through the door without detection.

They enter into a maze of hallways, and since they are not conversant in Chinese, it is difficult for them to know where they want to go. They have no knowledge of the Chinese language, whether Mandarin, Cantonese, or any other dialect that may be commonplace in northern China.

Heading down one of the larger hallways in a westerly direction, they thinks that they should snoop into each room as they come to it.

They enter the first room on the left, which appears to be an administrative office with a large number of c busy working away with paper. Upon closer examination it appears to be an accounting area of the operation. There is no excitement here, so they move down the hall to what holds promise of more interesting things. As it turns out, it is a staff lounge and much chit-chat abounds, not to mention there are a couple of love birds nestled in one corner engaging in the start of what is likely to develop into more than innocent petting.

Continuing down the hall they, come upon an active corridor, with a lot of military brass coming and going into the various office spaces.

Jake thinks really hard about how Koidon was able to change his language to English when they first met in Naranna. Koidon once stated that they would develop that skill in time. Jake is aware of his ability to speak European languages and is hopeful this talent extends to the asian languages, given his lack of testing his ability to speak any of the Chinese languages. He listens carefully to a conversation, and finally, his brain begins adapting to the language's logic, its sing-song pitches, and emphases, and in no time, Jake starts to comprehend. Wow, he thinks, this is handy and will make the journey a whole lot easier.

He overhears conversations about the family lives of the people, or the lack of it— how they have been abruptly stationed in this isolated location. These comments pique Jake's, interest as something new and important is happening.

Jake mentions to Maggie the secret of unlocking the language barrier and urges Maggie to try and achieve comprehension of the Chinese language. Maggie smiles and gives Jake the thumbs up; she, too, has mastered the language.

Entering another hallway, they come upon an elevator, but they think that it would be wise not to use the elevator until someone else uses it. A small group of people push the down button and enter the elevator. Jake and Maggie follow suit. One of them presses the button marked "U-9", the elevator doors close, the elevator and speeds to the requested floor. Filing out of the elevator behind the group of employees, they get a real surprise.

"General Whitmore, Major Hall, sir. We have scant

news coming from the stealth re-con mission. Moments ago, the Stealths were clearing the communication block zone around China and relayed this short message before they disappeared off our radar:

OMAHA S...

"Is that it, Major?"

"Yes, sir. Sir, the Eagle's Nest spotted and followed a couple of heat seeking missiles coming out of the communications block zone. Given their flight path, it was conjectured they were launched from Fuzhou just as the Stealths were about to cross the Tropic of Cancer. Our stealths were intercepted and presumed, downed, sir. We had no time to communicate or warn the pilots; it happened so quickly. I can only conclude that China has waged war."

General Whitmore grabs the red phone. "Mr. President, we have just received word that the stealth bombers have been shot down in the South China Seas near the Tropic of Cancer. Before they were blown off the radar by heat seeking missiles, they relayed the better part of two words: Omaha S... Sir, we can only assume that the USS *Omaha* was sunk, given the disappearance of our stealth bombers."

"General Whitmore, we will all gather at the White House in one hour. Loni will be in touch with the member's, and by the way, bring Major Hall."

"Yes, sir."

Again, the Joint Chiefs of Staff, the NSA, the CIA, and others are hustling into the war room. There is still little information to go on. Still, the communications lines are down.

Admiral Ewing appears shaken, having learned that the *Omaha* it is believed to have been sunk, and the lack of feedback to determine the fate of the crew rests heavily on his mind.

The president and Loni enter and the room becomes instantly hushed.

"Gentlemen, we appear to be at war with China! Loni, were you able to make contact with the Chinese Embassy?"

"No, sir, their telephone lines are not in service. Security also confirms that the embassy was vacated sometime within the last twenty-four hours."

"Well, it looks like those yellowbellies have defied protocol. They couldn't take the potential heat either and ran. Admiral Ewing, what is the plan for the Seventh Fleet?" the president inquires.

"Sir, the entire Seventh Fleet is now underway heading toward Batan in the Philippine Sea. Our two atomic-powered subs are heading toward South Korea and will await instructions just outside the communications cold zone near the Tropic of Cancer. This will position us strategically to strike any major military target or political target in mainstream China. Our plan is to not enter communications cold zone sea space until we are ready to execute our war plan. Their E.T.A. is approximately seventeen hours from now, sir."

Jake and Maggie can hardly believe their eyes. They have entered a huge underground cavern that is loaded with computers, computer monitors, and what looks like a thousand white coat engineers and scientists scurrying around as if their environment were afire.

Not wanting to be detected, they move into lesser traveled portions of the cavern. At every turn, there is something to bring shock and terror to their faces. It looks like the Chinese Military is in urgent deployment. The monitors display every deployment of troops, equipment, ships, aircraft, and missiles.

"Holy shit, Maggie, I don't believe it, but it appears China is invading; but invading what?"

"I can't make it out either, Jake. It's all like a large video game and, at the moment, seems unconnected."

"Whoa," Jake says, "regrouping and getting our bearings in here is the only way we are going to get a

178

logical and meaningful handle on what all this means."

Jake and Maggie spend the next hour moving around and listening in on various conversations. A small group of men is watching the fall of what looks like a parliament or legislative assembly. Red Army troops storm a building and mercilessly slay everyone in their path of destruction. Cheers arise from the group when the Army breaks down the barriers to a legislative assembly hall and massacres all who are there. Absolute mayhem, slaughter of defenseless humans— the monitors are just full of displays of atrocities. These scenes are horrifying to them, but to the assigned personnel, it is purely pleasurable. They can see it in their faces. After much planning, the successful execution of such plans is like receiving candy as the fruits of their efforts.

"This is no video game, Darling. This is the real thing, and it is happening now, as we speak. Jesus Christ, there must be some sense to this somewhere. It all seems beyond me."

"Get a grip, Jake. We can't crash now."

"You're right; let's move on."

More happy commotion occurs a little to the left of them. On the large computer monitors, a bevy of missiles are shown to be exploding, each intended target displayed in vivid details. In each case, it appears that political targets are being hit, with major destruction shown in every scene. Evidence abounds of people dying, and the walking wounded are in utter and disorientation.

Various military installations come under attack, evidence of which is seen through footage displayed on the monitors. Tanks, light and heavy artillery, planes, and war ships are being hammered with an endless barrage of incoming missiles. It appears that China has launched many offences, but without more insight as to the locations of the offences, it all remains unclear to Jake and Maggie.

They continue to push further through the cavern, looking for the perpetrator of these actions. All they are able to find here is the monitoring of hundreds of atrocities

179

currently underway, but they are still unable to identify where the aggressive action is taking place.

They move beyond the main cavern and into what appears to be a central control room. They spot General Xaing engaging in a heated but hushed roundtable discussion with his underlings. Each person around the table has a small monitor in front of him. Every so often, each person will cheer and then get back to the hushed debate or, at times, continue his armchair strategy of war that each of them seems to be preoccupied with.

Jake and Maggie move closer to the table in order to hear the conversation. Suddenly, General Xaing leaps to his feet and faces them. His face turning a ruddy red color, he says, "They are here. I can sense their presence. I must silence them at once, or my plans will be exposed."

Those around the table quickly stand and look in the direction of General Xaing. They look back at each other and share confusing looks. Jake and Maggie do not move and only have hopes that General Xaing will back off, but he moves closer, closer still, and then walks through them. He turns, looking carefully, then draws his 9-millimeter and fires off a magazine of rounds.

Major Hall continues to look for answers relating to the communications block that persists over much of Asia and Iran. A close watch of the two rogue satellites continues, as they now appear to be dormant again.

"I will not give into that theory again," Major Hall thinks. "Somehow, someone has developed the ability to transmit without detections, perhaps transmitting with the satellite's own protective shields."

Within their own protective shield— why didn't he think of that before? He couldn't answer. Yes, he thinks, that might explain how the satellites were launched and directed into position without the Eagle's Nest detection in the first place.

He begins to drum up all kind of variations of that

thought as Captain Willis yells with excitement, "Alpha 15 is picking up a clear signal of Iran. Sir, as Alpha 15 neared Iranian airspace, the snow and wavy lines lessened and then it began transmitting clear signals."

There is a hush and then a lot of excitement in the Eagle's Nest at this moment; however, no one dares leave his post to view the sweet screen.

"It still remains a mystery, and we have an urgent need to get to the bottom of it. Major Willis, I have been thinking along the lines that the rogue satellites have been transmitting within their own protective shields. We have not been able to view or pick up communications with those two satellites, nor were we aware of their existence until they were safely tucked into their orbit. Sir, we will kick that topic around. Perhaps it will spawn additional ideas or lead us to looking into this mystery differently. The president will be pleased, I think, that communications are back in Iran. I need to bring everyone up to date… General Whitmore, we have a positive development with respect to Iran, sir"

"Go ahead, Major."

"Sir, Alpha 15 is now receiving clear signals over Iran."

"Bravo, that is indeed good news. How did we resolve this issue and what is the status over Asia?"

"Sir, the clearing of the signals just happened, sir. We are no closer to understanding what is behind these events."

"Ugh!"

"Major, my most recent discussion with the president tells me, by the change in his voice, that he is getting very impatient."

"Yes, sir, we are highly concerned. We do not have the answers for the president. We are hoping for a breakthrough any moment."

"Major, what about Mr. Lee in Bangkok? Have we had any communications with him since his dispatch?"

"No, sir, he is currently about two hours behind in

getting back to us. We have been unable to reach him. We can only assume that he has run into some difficulties entering or exiting China. We will bide him more time; he is a very competent operative, possessing many superb skills."

Jake and Maggie breathe a sigh of relief, because they have escaped injury on account of General Xaing's 9-millimeter. It is time to move, as they have found the nerve centre and the operations room. They are still unable to put the puzzle together, as a computable explanation regarding the two satellites, their purpose, and the mystery that surrounds them seems incomplete.

Getting out of the control centre proves more difficult than they anticipated, as General Xaing is still ranting out of control. He is now demanding that infrared scanners be brought in immediately.

Jake turns to Maggie, and via mental telepathy, they agree to exit immediately via another parallel split universe. Maggie is sure this is possible and gets busy making this all happen.

They hold hands and are jettisoned from the control centre to another heavily secured large and noisy facility. With sirens blaring, security personnel scrambling and warning lights flashing, Jake and Maggie know that all the commotion is due to their presence being suspected by General Xaing. The ease of their movements will now be restricted with this heightened sense of security, as the whole staff is on high alert, looking for anything out of the ordinary. They have had some previous experience with this, and they are aware that they create drafts, that their scent follows them, and that, to highly sensitive individuals, their images may be all but visible, as the vibes that they emit create unwanted curiosity.

Like stealth vehicles, they begin to explore this strange environment, thinking that this is likely the secret covert space operation that they have been striving so hard to find. Activities in this space are very different from what they have previous encountered. Not wanting to risk their exposure, they view the computer screens from a distance, using their telescopic vision. They soon discover that this is the command centre for the two rogue satellites. One computer screen focuses on the continual stabilization of their orbits. Another screen projects the image of a silo seemingly from the underground base where they are situated and displays the maintenance of the connections to the satellites. It also displays straight lines intersecting with wavy lines and orbital lines alternating the lengths of their loops. Jake and Maggie simply cannot fathom the significance of the lines and shrug. A third screen appears to display the intensity of the output of signals from the satellites. This is purely and simply odd stuff for Jake and Maggie, but they know that they have hit pay dirt, so to speak.

Maggie zooms in a little more closely to the monitor screen that reads "Plasma Fusion Electro-Magnetic Field Injection Control Sensor."

"Jesus, Jake. Zoom in on the left monitor. What do you make of it?"

"I don't profess to know much about this science stuff, Maggie."

"I do recall a discussion at the White House regarding some speculation that the satellites were casting a web like block via an electro-magnetic field, but combining it with plasma fusion might just create the situation that is before us."

"This might explain the straight and wavy lines on the computer screen. Perhaps it symbolizes the transmission of the Plasma Fusion Electro-Magnetic Field."

"Great observation, Maggie. Let's not lose sight of this bit of information."

Jake spies a computer disk on the desk on which the monitor measuring the plasma fusion inputs is. As the desk is devoid of human occupation, Jake walks over and pockets the disk.

They know they are onto something really important and feel confident that they will now be able to locate and confirm the extent of the covert operations.

Maggie slips off to the far south corner of the room and suddenly becomes aware that there are six additional computer screens, each displaying additional satellites. Maggie motions to Jake to come over and look at these screens. Jake quickly confirms the existence of six additional satellites, making a total of eight satellites that will obviously be used to block world communications.

"Jesus, this is far more threatening than we once perceived," Jake thinks.

Having gained a better sense of their surroundings and the purpose of this centre, they decide to move in the direction of a disturbing noise. They really need to see the guts of this operation to be able to relate what they see to others when the time comes. "After all," they think, "we are only the runners. We are not the defenders." They know that their mission is to be the eyes and ears and communicators for the good of all.

Major Hall intercepts a coded message from Ono, another operative stationed out of Vietnam. As the decoders are busy unscrambling the message, Major Hall alerts Colonel Britch and General Whitmore of the incoming message. The coded message reads:

RAGONONODGNIPEELREOFTHESAWEBGNIN
UTHOFNANOSANIHCGDENTERINELLIKEEL

Captain Willis's team begins unscrambling the message in accordance with the Asian operative's current penning instructions. They set up a sixty-four square grid and start filling the grid from the top, left to right, until the grid is filled with letters. To read the message one must start at the bottom right, read left to right, and alternate left to right and keep alternating until he advances through the rows, with the end of the message ending at the far right of the top row. Major Hall reads the message aloud:

LEE KILLED ENTERING CHINA SOUTH NEAR NANNING.
BEWARE OF THE SLEEPING DRAGON. ONO

"Gentlemen," Major Hall states, "it seems that we are unable, at this time, to penetrate China's space. Lee's loss is a significant blow to the region's security. His skills will be difficult to replicate. Lee, rest in peace."

They sit in silence for a few minutes, and General Whitmore grimaces. He is in dire need of informing the president of the situation.

Jake and Maggie find themselves in a missile silo, which houses the massive equipment that is supplying the plasma fusion electro-magnetic field. They begin to scope out the silo and mentally pinpoint its location in relation to the base. They know they have found precisely what they were looking for, and now they need to head back to the monitoring stations that are displaying the atrocities of what they now believe is real warfare. They know that they have to identify the theatres of war somehow. With the communication blockages over much of Asia, they know that they will become the communicators, but they have not determined how, given the fact that they are truly unknown entities.

Safely navigating their way back to the monitoring stations, they think among themselves about their plan of action. Maggie notices an electronic map of Asia on the far wall at the end of the room that they are in. Upon closer examination, she sees that the map covers North and South Korea, Taiwan, Japan, Tibet and China itself. China is green and the other countries are red, with the exception of Tibet, which is orange. They study this map with interest, suspecting that what they witnessed earlier was the invasion and overthrow of the countries in red and that perhaps, in Tibet, the Chinese are targeting its many dissenters. They think that, given the massive number patriots, China's advance has to be more precise and protracted to prevent a heavy amount of Chinese civilian casualties. Jake suggest that they should confirm this theory by locating the screens that are set up to monitor the incursion of Tibet.

This is a very large facility, so a plan of attack is necessary in order to find the screens monitoring Tibet. Searching frantically to locate the screens, they hear a roar erupting amid the young engineers off to the right of their current position. They hurry over to see that much anticipated activity that is taking place.

The Red Army has smashed open the gates leading to the Great Temple where some of the Dalai Lama followers are housed. The screen now shows, in living action, the slaughter of many young holy men and many other supporters that are currently residing in or visiting the temple. With a bazooka-type shoulder mount, the temple doors are blown off their ancient hinges as if they were made of balsa wood.

Oh my god, Maggie exclaimed the Chinese are attacking the dissidents as we thought!

The Dalai Lama manages the government of Tibet from his exiled home in India. Although exiled from his mother country, he and some of his followers are busy conducting government business in an attempt to once again regain Tibet's independence. He has become quite puzzled and extremely agitated, having suddenly lost all communications with his Tibetan followers and now knows his followers must be in some imminent danger as a result. While having only once since his disposition to India made a short covert appearance in L'Hasta, he now knows he needs to repeat this act to ensure his followers safety. After much soul-searching, the Dalai Lama makes the difficult decision to return to the temple in L'Hasta under the cover of darkness with the aide of an experienced companion in this type of operation.

Gaining an understanding from his followers about

the increased pressure mounting on them by the Chinese government, the Dalai Lama suddenly realizes that his timing for a visit is about to become a case of survival of the fittest.

Red Army troops storm the temple, causing certain mayhem, death, and destruction. In the inner sanctum, behind steel doors, the Dalai Lama quickly prepares to vacate the facility via a secret tunnel directly accessible from behind the huge wall bookcase. With the Red Army directing smashing blows to the inner sanction steel door, access to the tunnel is gained. Now that he is safely entering the tunnel and activating the dim lighting, the heavy bookcase begins to close. Moments later, the inner sanctum door gives way, and the lead officer of the Red Army witnesses the wall closing and jams the bookcase so that a seal cannot be made.

The Dalai Lama and his most inner circle of associates are completely unaware of their own impending peril. They scurry down the dimmed tunnel, maintaining a quiet focus and putting as much distance between them and the Red Army as possible.

The Dalai Lama, having never had a reason to traverse this tunnel, knows it will lead him to safety, but the distance that they will have to travel is a mystery. What they might encounter along the way has not entered into the equation, as he feels that he is being looked after well. They come to a fork in the tunnel with no indication of which way they should seek. The Dalai Lama thinks hard about all his learned wisdom dealing with tense escape situations, admits to himself that it is not much, and then recalls the words once said to him by one of his great ancestors: "Humans are gifted with both Logic and Creativity, thus developing a balance between the two is essential for survival. Creativity is the intuition that leaves us free to leave the comfortable pew of what we know, promoting the health, development, and growth of our mind. Logic assembles and characterizes data, vision, and emotion, leading one to an enriched conclusion. If Right is

187

Left and Left is Right, then one can assume that two Rights make a Left. Follow your intuition and logic!" So, he decides to use the left yawing tunnel. His instinct suggests that the right tunnel is a fool's tunnel that will come to an abrupt end, with the footing giving way, thus creating a fall of hundreds of feet that will bring him a certain and untimely death.

Continuing the journey with renewed confidence, they quicken the pace but keep a vigilant eye on what lies ahead. The air begins to cool, and they start to feel a light breeze on their faces, so they know that they are nearing the exit point of the first stage of their escape. Slowing their pace to a mere crawl, they inch their way in much anticipation of their own detection.

The Dalai Lama, having not previously taken the time to research the escape route, seems somewhat less confident about what his expectations are once they are exposed to the external elements. This slight hesitation combines with what sounds like frantic screams for help from within the tunnel, and then, silence sends shock waves of fear over them. Once they exit the tunnel, they survey the hillsides around them and above. To their relief, they feel alone and isolated in this rugged mountainous landscape.

Believing not all their pursuers have succumbed to a certain and known fate, anticipating some soldiers are likely behind, them they scurry up and down the Sum Shih Trail in the Himalaya Mountains, seeking safe refuge near Ledo. A considerable distance needs to be traversed prior to crossing the mountainous Tibetan border. The trail, very seldom used over the past half-century, is over grown with small bushes, and many parts have been eroded by the tough and brutal summer-winter weather cycles. Slogging at best at times, gaining distance between them and their pursuers seems to be an insurmountable task.

With no advanced warning, they hear a pulsating fump-whump-whumping sound. Suddenly, a gunship helicopter rises up above them, cresting the hillside, then menacingly landing in the wake of its own dust storm. Six Chinese soldiers quickly exit from the helicopter with automatic weapons in their hands and demand that the Delia Lama and his small following hit the dirt, which they do without question. Exiting from the helicopter is a cameraman, who begins to set up his equipment. No further communication existing, the soldiers hold their weapons on their quarry. The Dalai Lama and his followers lay in sheer desperate anticipation of their fate. The commanding officer then orders the Dalai Lama and his followers to stand and form a line in front of him. He ensures that the Dalai Lama is in the centre of the line.

Jake and Maggie again hear the jubilant shouts from the engineers observing the Screen in Tibet and quickly move over to observe the new activity. To their shock they are now looking at the Dalia Lame and a small group of his followers facing what now appears to be a firing squad. The officer in charge, conferring with the cameraman to ensure that he is ready and filming, turns to the Dalai Lama and states, "We did not anticipate your presence, so now it is my honor and duty to bring about quick justice to you and your followers. You and your followers are religious traitors…"

The computer screen abruptly develops a snow-white appearance followed by a heavy static noise. Communications are lost for the moment. A horrifying hush overcomes the once robust and merry sounds in the monitoring room, and an extreme measure of disappointment is evident, as those present are not able to officially confirm their victory.

General Xaing comes roaring into the monitoring room, yelling expletives at those managing the screens. He demands an explanation for the screens' failure and immediately threatens the head engineer with his 9-

millimeter. The head engineer, unable to explain, indicates that all systems are checking out all right and suggests that there is a difficulty on the actual site itself. General Xaing lowers his 9-millimeter from the engineer's head and mutters that that is a credible response.

General Xaing, in his haste, exclaims victory over Tibet in spite of no hard proof, and summons his commanding officers for the implementation of Phase II of their plan of attack.

CHAPTER 29
Plans

Back at home, Jake and Maggie just hug each other, knowing that, at least for the moment, they are safe, but little comfort is afforded them just knowing what is apparent. The rest of the world is not aware. Yes, there is the realization that those people living in countries overtaken by China are now living in a certain hell, not knowing whether or not they will survive the attacks of aggressor. The rest of the world is oblivious to their plight and their own impending plight. If they only knew, Jake thinks.

They turn on the TV to CNN to get a glimpse of the world news. Not to their surprise, there is no mention of what the have just witnessed.

Jake and Maggie know that they have to take an initiative, and quickly, before the Chinese are able to execute the second and most ambitious stage of their plan.

"Maggie, we must get to Washington with all God's speed."

"What are you planning on doing, Jake?"

"I just had an insight. I now know that the president is about to meet with his Joint Chiefs of Staff, the CIA, Global Protector, Homeland Security, and the NSA. It is imperative that we interrupt that meeting and present our findings. This is the only way that we can assist them, even if it means certain risk for ourselves."

"Jake, we can't just appear during their meeting. We will surely be arrested, and who will ever believe us?"

"I know that we just can't barge in, but somehow we need to get their attention quickly and provide them with some real evidence that they can grasp. They are buffaloed, after all, and are desperate for a break through. We need to provide that break through and establish a level of credibility and, at the same time, become influential. I have a strong sense that now is the time that I should bring Koidon into the picture. We will need his help."

"Jake, what about you father? Wouldn't this be an appropriate time to bring him in, too? Remember, Jake, your father is working on behalf of the Higher Power, and he has been providing you with some guidance from the get-go of this mission."

"You're right, Maggie. Now would be the perfect opportunity. One: It might give us the confidence to move on, and secondly, he may share additional insights. Having all of us together on one spot to plan our next move is a terrific idea. Thanks, Sweetie."

There is so much to plan in a very limited timeframe. Jake starts to wonder if he can actually summons Koidon to his home. If this is possible, the planning can be completed much faster and they can be better coordinated in their execution. Jake attempts to communicate with Koidon via mental telepathy. Having not tried this before, he doesn't really think that the process of connecting might be different, given the fact that they are in different parallel universes.

Koidon finally responds to Jakes frantic pleas, and they carry on a short conversation among themselves. Jake turns to Maggie and alerts her to the fact Koidon will be appearing in just a few moments. Jake now focuses his attention on summoning his dad. He is so impressed at how successful he was with Koidon that he expects to have the same success with his dad. Jake and his dad connect in thought, and they arrange to meet. Jake rather pleased with himself indicates to Maggie the meeting will now be complete, as his father has agreed to attend.

Koidon's arrival brings tears to Maggie's eyes. She just feels so relieved that they are no longer alone in this hideous adventure. She is so happy to see him again, because not only does she like him, but also she loves what he and his civilization stand for. Koidon gives Maggie a big four-armed hug upon his arrival. A real bond is apparent between the three of them as Koidon extends one of his hands to Jake.

Jake's father's arrival is an historic event for the Bloomingdales. Tear flowed like giant waterfalls cascading down a majestic, gigantic mountainside. After a real warm welcome, Jake's father is introduced to Koidon. As it turns out, no introductions are necessary. Jake's father and Koidon embrace as if they were long lost buddies waiting in great anticipation of this visitation. One can see and feel a great connection between them, as if sometime in their past or perhaps even in their recent past they entrusted each other with life's mysteries.

Maggie and Jake stare in awe at the sight of Koidon and Jake's father embracing in such an emotional reunion. Such a heartfelt unification and display of admiration toward each other would lead any viewer to acknowledge that they both are formidable warriors who have fought similar battles in the past and now, at long last, can celebrate those victorious moments.

Maggie, still standing in awe, can only muster a meager offering of a cup of blackberry herbal tea and a few not-so-homemade, store-bought peanut butter cookies to Koidon and Jake's father.

Koidon has never before made a visit to their home and states how impressed he is with their living space and surroundings. He feels quite comfortable here with Jake and Maggie and misses seeing Katey very much.

Jake's father is also very impressed with the elegant décor exhibited throughout the home.

"You have mastered the art of carpentry and design, son, and you have accomplished so much since your humble beginnings. I am so pleased to have this opportunity to come back and witness your accomplishments."

Unfortunately, they all know that there isn't much

time for small talk, as the world's situation is worsening by the minute. Sitting around the kitchen island, they begin to devise a game plan. First, they agree that it is mandatory to get Washington up and running, not to mention helping them to gain confidence and creditability in them. Second, they discuss and agree to a plan that will include Koidon and his civilization, as it is well-known that Koidon's special and unearthly talents will be definitely needed.

Jake's father has concerns that Jake and Maggie should not make themselves known to those who are attending the meeting for security reasons. He also suggests that all the shock and awe they can muster will heighten their interest and perhaps trust. Only information that is factual and, where possible, assumed secret shall be presented. Jake's father indicates his pleasure in being included but declines the offer to attend and participate in the meeting.

"The Higher Power supports my presence here and now; however, my role and focus is in Meadowbrook. You will do well. You are the best team I know of. Good luck."

Having invested an hour of good planning time, the three of them who remain decide that it is time to visit the White House, more precisely the Presidential Meeting Room at the White House.

They stand around the kitchen island and all join hands. Koidon takes the lead, and instantly they arrive in the Presidential Meeting Room.

A hot, intense meeting is well underway, with each major actor accusing the other of incompetence. It is readily apparent that they are still in the dark as to what is happening in the real world.

Jake quickly walks past the president, ensuring that a mild gust of air stirs and raises his ire. He needs to break the tense atmosphere in the room, thus giving him a few moments to create happenings, however paranormal.

The president yells out, "Silence. I believe we have been infiltrated, gentlemen. I have felt the presence of an individual or individuals in this room before, and I now feel that presence again. General Whitmore, do you feel a presence?"

"Yes, sir, but for some unexplained reason, I sense that this presence is not to be feared."

"General Whitmore, have you gone soft? Is age mellowing you out? How can you sense the difference between good and evil, General?"

"I just don't feel any anxiety associated with this medium exchange. It feels natural, sir."

"Call security now," the president yells out.

NO!

The word "no", in black bold print, slowly appears on the blackboard.

What the hell is going on?" the president states in a startling, bellowing roar. "Look at the board, General."

All eyes turn toward the board.

The words "OHAMA SUNK, YES," appear on the board. Jake is now starting to have some fun, writing short messages and perhaps toying with their minds. Not one person moves. All are wide-eyed, drop-jawed, and speechless. "THE FATE OF THE DALAI LAMA IS UNKNOWN, BUT HE IS IN IMMINENT DANGER," appears on the board. The audience is captivated and spellbound, clearly unable to respond, riveted to their seats, aghast. Jake isn't sure when to play his open hand, as he does not trust the actions or re-actions of those around the table. The message is so critical that he cannot risk for a second to not be heard. The survival of the world, he knows, rests on the actions of the next few moments. Jake turns to Koidon, seeking silent approval that what he was doing is all right. Koidon, via mental telepathy, suggests that he speak about the eight satellites and the communications black out. *This action will surely reduce them to putty in your hand, Jake.* Jake scribes the following message on the board:

TWO SATELLITES, IN ELLIPTICAL ORBIT, CASTING A

195

COMMUNICATIONS BLACK OUT VIA PLASMA FUSION
ELECTRO-MAGNETIC FORCE FIELD, ARE THE GOLDEN KEY TO
THIS PERPLEXING WORLD DRAMA. SIX ADDITIONAL
SATELLITES HAVE BEEN DEPLOYED TO ENSURE WORLDWIDE
COMMUNICATIONS BLOCKS SOON.

The president leaps into the communications volley. "That is simply not true. There are only two satellites in elliptical orbit, and I have difficulty understanding your knowledge of their existence."

Jake writes:

ONLY FACTS AND INFORMATION OF RELEVANCE ARE
COMMUNICATED BY US. EAGLE'S NEST WILL CONFIRM
WHEN THEIR CURRENT SURVEILLANCE IS COMPLETE!
BALLISTIC MISSILES WERE LAUNCHED PRIOR TO THE
STEALTH BOMBERS BEING SHOT DOWN. THEIR IDENTITIES
WERE MISTAKEN; SIX SATELLITES WERE LAUNCHED AND
ARE NOW IN THEIR DESIGNATED ORBIT.

Jake reached in his pocket and removes the computer disk that he took from the desk in the plasma fusion control room and carefully places it on the table in front of the president. Distancing himself from the disk, Jake thinks hard about releasing it from the split universe that he is in and having it materialize in the president's universe. The disk oddly appears from nowhere in front of the president, which takes him by complete surprise.

Jake writes this message next:

THIS DISK CONTAINS THE SECRET TECHNOLOGY BEHIND THE
COMMUNICATIONS BLACK OUT, WITH OUR COMPLIMENTS.

Loni thrusts open the meeting room doors, bursting in with a beseeching look on her face and a message in her quaking, slender, soft hand.

"Mr. President, this strange message just arrived on your secure monitor. It's odd, sir, but there is no trace of who sent this message or where it came from."

"Um, it makes little sense to me. Obviously it is written in code. With what's been going on lately, I sense it is of utmost importance. Loni, get the decoders on this now."

"Sir, I have already alerted the NSA, and they are on their way.'

The decoders from the pentagon arrive and review the contents of the message:

AEAVEOPYRTADIRRESYTRECALAUOETCTLDCRUNHLOL
PERRTCARNRFEAIHRYEDUNROIEOWELDMNNSYWRLES

"Mr. President, we have great capabilities in cracking any code with our new decoding program Crack-It. It will take some time to run this through our computer, sir, but we will be back as soon as possible."

The president shift's his attention to the message on the board.

"How the hell did this get out? Someone has been leaking out information, General. The presence of the two satellites is a secret. How is it possible that they, or whoever it is present here, have knowledge that we do not have?"

General Whitmore, not having an answer to that posed question, remains silent, and a shade of white pales his face.

Sitting there in an absolute state of disbelief, the president says, "Whatever you are, or whoever you are, what other messages do you have? Reveal yourselves. Quit jerking us around?"

Jake again begins to scribe the following:

PREPARE THE ATOMIC SUBS WITH DEEP PENETRATING MISSILES HEADS. THE TARGET IS 140 FEET BELOW GROUND SURFACE. THE COORDINATES ARE LONGITUDE 124.62, 31 MINUTES, LATITUDE 48.28, 03 MINUTES. GIVEN YOUR IMPENDING LACK OF COMMUNICATIONS, ONCE THE

MISSILES ENTER THE COMMUNICATIONS COLD AREA, YOU
MUST ENSURE THE PRESET COORDINATES.

"General Whitmore," the president states,
"logistically reference that location on out world mapping
program."

"Yes, sir. Sir, the location is 3.75 miles due north of
Nenjiang."

"Get the NSA to send over their satellite photos
depicting those coordinates and now."

"Sir, done as we speak!"

Maggie decides to add a bit of spice to the meeting
by circling some countries on the wall in red. She circles
North Korea, South Korea, Japan, Taiwan, and Tibet.
Those sitting around the table are awed by the event that is
currently taking place.

Maggie then writes:

HOW MANY IN THE ROOM WOULD HAVE BEEN SURPRISED
AT THIS OUTCOME?

There is a long silent pause, and the question
remains unanswered.

The president says, "What does that mean?"

Then she writes "CHINA— TODAY?"

The president inquires, "Are we to believe that
China has invaded those circled countries and now
occupies them?"

"YES."

"Who are you, and why should we believe you?"

Koidon suddenly appears before the group, slipping
out from behind his split parallel cover.

Jaws again drop; beads of sweat appear on the
brows of those sitting; and many squirm in angst. The
horrid physical presence of Koidon is more than some can
handle. Loni, having the most difficulty, faints in her chair.
Loni recovers slowly, only with the warm   reassuring
stroking of the president's hand on her back. Having this

perfectly horrid creature standing before them knocks them so far off balance that none can muster the courage or strength to utter a word. Yes, intense fear overtakes the great warriors of America.

Koidon speaks softly but firmly. "Gentlemen and lady, it is not my intention to frighten you. This is how I look, and I make no apology! There isn't sufficient time for me to explain who I am or where I have come from. You can bet it is not Earth. My people and I live in a parallel universe in South America. My two Canadian friends and I have grave concerns that the wonderful world we live in will forever change should you not take swift action immediately. We have provided you with some critical information, which will assist you. We have shared information about the satellites and have identified the source and type of force being used to create convenient communications black outs, which you know is highly privileged and secret information. We have come in peace to alert you to what you could not have known, given your simple human shortcomings. There is no slight intended. It is a simple fact. China is about to play its trump card, and the world will belong to them. You have a choice: You can believe us and use this information to do whatever is necessary for this event not to happen, or you can not believe us and continue to be blinded by your arrogance and simple intelligence. It is your choice to make. We are only the providers— the eyes, the ears.

"I, Koidon, leader of my civilization, will not sit back and allow the destruction of the world as we now know it. However, it is not for me or my people to carry out your work, but we might assist you should it become necessary. We have much to do and so little time to do it in. We will leave you now. We trust that you will do the right thing and maintain your world dominance, as it's for the good of all."

"General Whitmore," Koidon states pointedly, "I expect no thanks, but my people seized an opportunity that night in Iran, when the gunship was blown up, and intervened by gently bringing its crew back to ground. Call it a divine intervention or a freak of nature or perhaps a paranormal experience, but believe it."

Koidon returns to join Jake and Maggie in the split universe. Koidon, Jake, and Maggie huddle together and soon disappear from the Presidential Meeting Room and arrive back at the Bloomingdales' residence.

Over a cup of cranberry herbal tea, they engage in a rehash of this day's event. Soon they are discussing their personal game plans to assist the Americans meet their intended or expected objective.

Koidon gives Maggie a big four-armed hug and shakes Jake's hand, and after saying goodbye, he disappears back to his homeland to return to his loved ones and to be sure and confident about what role he and his people must and will play.

CHAPTER 30
Another Discovery

Captain Willis and his team are watching new developments appear on their monitoring screens. Captain Willis immediately identifies two new satellites in elliptical orbits. Alerting Major Hall, he confirms that they now have four satellites for which they can't account.

"Call me in five minutes with an update, Captain."

"Yes, sir."

Captain Willis and his team comb the skies, looking to determine the status of these new satellites, when four more are located. Now there are a total of eight in elliptical orbit, circling Earth. It is determined that there is enough capability in those eight satellites to continuously cover the entire world with a communications block.

Again, there is no trace of their origin. They simply and suddenly appear in place, as if they have been there forever.

"Major Hall," Captain Willis yells, "we have spotted six additional rogue satellites now solidly positioned in the familiar elliptical orbit. That brings a total up to eight unidentified satellites in our field of vision."

If these satellites are behind the communications block over Iran, and now over most of Asia, then Captain Willis suspects that there are sufficient satellites to block the entire world.

CHAPTER 31
Preparations

"Admiral Ewing, update us on the status of the Seventh Fleet," the president demands.

If it seemed like there were pleasantries in past communications, the ante has been upped; make no mistake about it. Be sharp, be crisp, or be cut to shreds.

"The entire fleet is in its staging position, sir. Given our experience with the communications block over Iran, the movement of the Seventh Fleet will likely not be noticed by the Chinese. I have commanded our two atomic subs, the USS *Shadow* and the USS *Prowler*, to set deep penetrating missile warheads and prepare the first silos for discharge. The arming of the missiles will be concluded in about thirty minutes from now."

"General Whitmore, update us on your tactical plan."

"Yes, sir. Once the ballistic missiles have been launched, we will immediately launch the first wave of aircraft. It is expected that, should the defined coordinates be correct, they will completely destroy the military base north of Nenjiang. The mysterious communications black out should lift and our aircraft should be able to navigate and maintain communications and target all known military installations. We expect the second wave of ballistic missiles to be launched and their intended targets are the other known military institutions and bases, political assemblies, and major government and party headquarters."

Loni leads Captain Pitt in from the Pentagon.

"Sir, we have successfully decoded the message it is..."

The president's red phone rings.

"Mr. President, it's Major Hall speaking, sir. Sir, we have now spotted eight unidentified rouge satellites, all in the same elliptical orbit. We have no record of their launch or trajectory arc. Both have apparently been blocked. It remains a complete mystery where these satellites are coming from. Something is preventing our initial detection, and this problem still requires a solution. We are not observing what we believe in a major development over Alaska and northern Canada. Thins are happening fast, sire. We believe the communications block is now stretching and making its way over North America... Correction, sir: We are now witnessing a communications black out starting to spread over northern Russia. Sir, as we speak, this is so much of Earth now being blackened out, and it is slowly rising from the South Pole as well. Sir, given the speed at which the webbing is encroaching, we estimate that there will be a complete worldwide communications black out within one hour."

"We're on it, Major, keep working on it from your end... Gentlemen, thank God we got the tip about the eight satellites from our new-found friends. It has given us the much-needed time to prepare ourselves. Captain Pitt, what was the content of that coded message?"

"Sir, given the simple nature of this code, we had little difficulty cracking it."

"Captain," the president flares back, "cut the crap. What does it say!"

"Sir, the message reads like this."

Captain Pitt then shows the president this diagram:

INADECLAR
HWORLDORE
CWSURREDS
HEYRARNEV
TNLUSMDRI
RLLOYREPC
ALUFECAET

EAREVOYRO
NOITNETTA

"In order to read the message," he continues, "you must start from the bottom right square and read right to left. Then, at the bottom left, read up until you get to the upper left hand square. Then, read left to right and then from the upper right hand square read down. You just repeat this process until you reach the center square, that being the end of the message. Thus, the message reads like this:

ATTENTION EARTH. CHINA DECLARES VICTORY OVER ALL
NEW WORLD ORDER. PEACEFULLY SURRENDER YOU ARMS."

The president decrees, "You can damn well bet we won't surrender. Not now. Not ever. Gentlemen, this is a declaration of war on the part of China, and we must respond in the only way we know. We must implement our war plan immediately. Gentlemen, man your battle stations and prepare for out engagement in war."

The White House opens its floodgates as the Army brass flee the complex to prepare themselves for their theater of war.

This quick turn of events catches the media off guard and leaves them only to wonder if this is it the end of the world. Is anyone home at the White House or what? It's the "or what" impetus that swings the media into action. They begin making contact with their connections around the world to get a handle on what is going on. Minute by minute the media discover that more and more of their contacts are now simply out of reach. The realization that fewer and fewer of their contacts can be reached causes panic in the media world.

While they are ethically bound only to report what is the truth, they simply do not know if the "what is" is or isn't, and they simply start to report their frustration of not knowing anything. The media's blithering catches the public's attention, cause them to realize that all may not be going as well as they assumed, and conversations begin to consume work places, homes, and various social arenas, stirring, for now, a gentle panic among the masses.

A mass demonstration of media interests fills the front grounds of the White House, demanding that they be let in on what atrocity has occurred in the world. Using megaphones and other pieces of amplified equipment, they generate sufficient noise and disruptions, leaving the president no option but to call in the National Guard to disperse the angry group.

The president, now more than fully consumed with the advent of war, turns his attention to the creeping worldwide communications black out. He instructs Loni to get in touch with the Prime Minister of Canada and the President of Mexico for a telephone conference.

"Be sure the telephone conference occurs on the ground secured lines."

Canada and Mexico have become close allies in the past year since the implementation of the NAEU (North American Economic Union). While Washington, D.C., has become the official Capital of North America under this agreement, due to population and world might, Ottawa, Canada has become the Northern Regional Capital, holding responsibilities of ensuring North American sovereignty over the Arctic and Northern Pacific and Northern Atlantic regions. The State of Alaska has been realigned and now comes under the auspices of the Canadian Regional Capital for administrative purposes only.

Mexico City, Mexico, likewise, has become the Southern Regional Capital and holds the responsibilities of ensuring the North American southern extremities as sovereign.

Loni enters the Oval Office and advises the president that the Prime Minister of Canada and the President of Mexico are now on hold awaiting the conference call.

"Thanks, Loni. By the way, with so much going on

and you spending so much time here, how is Bert holding up to all of this?"

Surprised, Loni says, "Thanks for asking, Mr. President. Oh, he is in his glory, sir. He is out to sea, just itching to let those engines roar, let those missiles soar, and make some heavy scores. He's still a kid at heart, sir. He'd rather be out there on some high seas adventure than be bored at home with me.'

"Yes, yes never lose the kid in you. Patch me into the conference call, Loni."

"Yes, sir."

The president briefs the two heads of state on the crisis and what is about to occur and receives confirmation that whatever is needed of their countries will be made available post haste.

The Canadian prime minister expresses surprise and shock that he was not taken into the president's confidence prior to the action being taken against China. He suggests that he will have some difficulty mustering his limited home based troops and aging equipment in the event that something woefully goes wrong and the war expands beyond the Chinese border and that he may need some assistance from the U.S. to defend the hundreds of miles of shorelines.

The president retorts that he has never had any expectations of Canada beyond accepting the Northern Missile Defense System and suggests that that be implemented with or without the approval of the dozy Senate. The consequences of dithering over the defense system can cost the Western World its superiority.

The president states "In the time of war, anything goes, and if there is a need to deploy missiles over Canada's airspace, so be it. I will worry about relationships later."

The Mexican president is also alarmed that the state of world affairs has progressed so far without his knowledge and chastises the President of the United States for withholding vital information that can have a profound impact on his country.

"Gentlemen, I offer no apologies. The national security of my country, and the security of the world for that matter, has been breached, and the stakes are so high that I have not been able to confer with any country worldwide. So, you should feel privileged that I am now sharing this with you, fully confident that this information remains solely with us for the time being. Stand by," the President of the United States demands.

CHAPTER 32
Showdown

At 12:01 EDT, the president issues the war orders. The two atomic subs move into the outer extremities of the communications black out zone and launch their first volley of deep penetrating missiles toward their intended target approximately 3.75 miles north of Nenjiang, China. It is calculated that the missiles will reach and destroy this target in fourteen minutes, thirty-two seconds. As the clock ticks, the subs prepare for the second launch of preset and predestined missiles, some intended toward the same target thus ensuring the complete destruction of the entire command headquarters and the others toward known political and large established military targets.

The USS *Kitty Hawk*, at 12:15 EDT, launches its first wave of bombers and fighter jets toward planned smaller military and political destinations.

At 12:16 EDT, the communications block suddenly disappears, signaling the fact that the missiles were successful in destroying their intended target and allowing the bomber and fighter jets to maintain communications and proceed toward their intended targets.

At 12:20 EDT, the USS *Saratoga* launches its first wave of bombers and fighter jets, set to undertake their targets in the southern portion of China.

At 12:21 EDT, the balance of the Seventh Fleet is given its orders to advance to within striking distance of the China coastal military establishment and other political targets.

The success of destroying the Northern Military Command Headquarters and covert space operations center and the restoration of the communications are being celebrated by the Seventh Fleet command.

News soon hits the White House and the president immediately summons his Joint Chiefs of Staff to report directly on the progress that is being made. There is a shift in the atmosphere around the White House now that some level of success has been immediately achieved and the mysterious communications block has now disappeared. The scowls and grim looks on the faces of the White House staff are now replaced with smiles on somewhat beaming faces.

The president, while waiting for his members to arrive begins, strutting and pacing the floor of the Oval Office, with chest held high, knowing that he has redeemed himself in the eyes of the world communities. He turns his attention to the new revelations about Iran, which the covert Secta-Iranian mission unearthed. He now has hardcore evidence of an atomic development and manufacturing facility, so he now needs to build a strategy for how and when to present these new findings to the U.N.

The timing couldn't be worse to go to the U.N. seeking actions against Iran's nuclear involvement, as he hasn't apprised them of his declaration of war against China. There wasn't time to listen to the U.N. hum and haw as to whether it was indeed time to serve an appropriate action. There is no time, at times, to wallow in the bureaucratic process. Sometimes it simply warrants guns a-blazing. In this situation, when it is believed that only one hour remains prior to China choking off worldwide communications and seizing control, becoming the new world order, it definitely warrants guns a-blazing.

The president thinks of the other discoveries found in Iran and how the combination of findings surely will support his bid for actions against Iran.

Another matter crosses his mind while awaiting the Joint Chiefs of Staff: the munitions shipments heading to New York City and Toronto, Canada. Homeland Security had better be apprised, and appropriate action had better be taken.

The Joint Chiefs of Staff file into the Presidential Meeting Room at the White House. There is a lighter and more humorous atmosphere, considering that some positive progress is being made with the incursion in China. A few outbursts of laughter can be heard, which gives the president a good feeling as he walks through the meeting room doors.

"Gentlemen, be seated," the president says with a boyish smile developing over his face. "I'm beginning to hear some good results. Bravo... General Whitmore would you please give us an update in your quarters."

"Yes, sir. The communications block that was about to engulf the entire world has been lifted, which indicates that our missiles were successful in destroying their intended targets. We have now heard from our re-con flight over the Base Headquarters near Nenjiang. We have scored direct hits there. There is nothing left to salvage and nary a sole is visible. No collateral damage occurred. The city of Nenjiang is intact, and it would appear that the local population is in some state of confusion as to what is happening. The Eagle's Nest reports that all satellites are performing at one hundred percent, and they have been able to zero in on a number of critical sites bombed during this mission. The main political headquarters, the Imperial Palace, and the Political Assembly have been totally destroyed. Again, these were direct hits, and little collateral damage occurred."

"Thank you, General. It sounds as if we may receive a surrender notification in the very near future... Admiral Ewing, report your activities in your theater of war."

"Sir, I won't repeat what General Whitmore has said, but we have received reports that all of the first wave missiles scored direct hits and that all but one in the second wave scored direct hits. One missile was a dud; however, our bomber mission was able to divert and destroy the intended target. Our bombers took out seventy-two major military and political installations, both inland and on the South China Sea coast. Our fighter planes downed forty-five enemy fighters, caused major damage to twelve military airports, and destroyed hundreds of military aircrafts. Sir, a recent report from the USS *Kitty Hawk* indicates that the fighters are no longer encountering resistance. Our losses to date are twelve fighter jets and two bombers."

"Sir," General Whitmore says, "I have just received a communication from Colonel Britch confirming the liberation of Taiwan. It's sad, sir, but it appears that all former political leaders were assassinated during this brief takeover. We have some good news, though, sir. Twelve hundred and forty-nine sailors from the USS *Omaha* have survived the sinking of their warship and are now in safe hands with a new provisional government.

"Sir," General Whitmore states, "a communication just received by the Eagle's Nest confirms that Japan has been liberated. The members of the royal family are safe and are now under the heavy guard of an elite division of the Japanese Air Force. Again, it appears that many of the political leaders were massacred during their brief takeover."

"Sir," Admiral Ewing says, "I have just received word from the USS *Bounty*, Destroyer Class. They are now anchored in the Yellow Sea. The ship's commander has been communicating with the South Korean government officials in Seoul, confirming that the Chinese have fled the country, returning to their homeland. South Korea has been liberated as a result of the AWOL status of the Red Army divisions assigned to South Korea. Some of the political leaders were assailed within the assembly; however, fortunately, very few members were present during the takeover; therefore, it is assumed that many have survived the incursio

"Sir," General Whitmore interjects, "another message of good news: Tibet is once about free as it ever was, as the Chinese invasion force has left that country and returned to China. It would appear the Chinese have abandoned all efforts to maintain governmental control of Tibet. Our satellite reports that the Great Temple and grounds have been invaded and not believed deserted. We are unaware of the status of the Dalai Lama and his followers at this time... Sir, an unconfirmed report has been received from one of our covert operatives stating that North Korea has also been freed. The status of the president's condition is unknown."

"Good work gentlemen," the president states with a smile and a sigh. "We have the mighty strength and the technical advantage to maintain our worldly status while inflicting a minimum of collateral damage. We will maintain our guard, and we will continue to fly over China to observe any changes to our current conditions. We will await, for the moment, any direct communication from China before we step foot on their soil. It continues to be America's intent to protect ourselves and maintain a profound interest in re-establishing relationships with China... General Whitmore, we need to address the U.N. with regard toward the recent events caused by China, and I think it is time to raise the issues concerning Iran. Get your boys working on our positions on China and Iran."

"Yes, sir. I am on it now."

"We shall meet in a couple of days," the President says. "Perhaps, by that time, we will have heard from China."

CHAPTER 33
Emerging Power

Within a twenty-four-hour period, a swift and powerful deathblow has been bestowed upon the Chinese Military Headquarter in Nenjiang. The collapse of their aero space program, the destruction of other strategic military units and sub command posts, and the complete destruction of the political establishment of the country have caused the newly awakened Sleeping Dragon to be once again silenced.

From the ashes created by the gladiators' war emerges swiftly and assuredly a new power from within. The new power of bright, young, and well-educated Chinese men and women spare no time in pledging a peace allegiance with the balance of the world. One is left to wonder if this well-organized group has been waiting for the right opportunity to arise and perform a safe and peaceful coup.

It doesn't matter. The Americans don't have any interest in occupying China. They just want to maintain their superiority in the world and are quite interested in developing a relationship with this unknown group, if in fact they represent the interests of the majority of Chinese people. A cautious and safe approach is determined, and they want to re-open the lines of communications.

They, the New Power, representing what is believed to be the general populous of China, are profoundly aghast at the actions taken against the world by their political predecessors and the military. They pledge and vow that China will immediately become a democratic nation, shedding their corruption and brutality toward other

213

humans, allowing for a more overt and economically productive nation. Communism is dead and gone forever.

The new self-appointed Power Group is quick to notice that the American aggression against their country was simply an act of self-defense. This belief and realization is broadcast throughout the country, and the world also acknowledges that the New China, China's People's Democracy, no longer believes in and will no longer recognize communism, and they will function as a democracy.

The new Provisional Leader of China places a telephone call to the President of the United States of America.

EPILOGUE

Jake and Maggie are finally relaxing in their Adirondack chairs in their back yard, with Maggie sipping a glass of white wine and Jake sipping a glass of red wine. Just after sunset, when the sky turns a beautiful crimson red in the West, they search the skies to the Northeast and to the Northwest, where they witness four pure white blinding laser flashes, and to the Southeast and Southwest, they also witness four white laser flashes illuminating the entire sky in a way that they have never seen before. It is such a wonderful sight for Jake and Maggie, as they know that Koidon and his people are executing the last act, destroying the eight rouge satellites. To others who bore witness to the events around the world, it brought fear, intrigue, and question. What is that all about? Are we as a world going into a meltdown, or is it a freak of nature? Most people, however, will just shrug it off as to another unexplainable occurrence. So what? Who cares? It didn't hurt or affect me.

Jake and Maggie again focus their attention toward the western skyline. The incredible vibrancy and brilliance of that deep crimson red sky interlacing with wispy cirrus clouds emanating from the recent sunset captivate and awe them. It is such a special evening of intense color, and the high cirrus clouds appear like angels softly and majestically swaying or dancing with delight while casting a red hue, giving them a living presence.

They are about to lift their glasses for a toast when they are surprised by an unexpected visit from a flock of whir-bits. The whir-bits fly within a few feet of them; hundreds of beady, black ebony eyes settle in for a moment of stillness, captivating their attention, and then, they flutter off and form the outline of two perfectly shaped, interlaced hearts.

They bring tears to their eyes, using the brilliant crimson red sky as a backdrop, reflecting the shimmering radiance of the once white, now red, wispy cirrus clouds. Jake always knew that the whir-bits' presence was a good omen, but he didn't know that they were so capable of creating such an immense emotional presence.

The whir-bits then break the double heart formation, regroup into a V-like formation, and then soar past Jake and Maggie, executing a precise "V" for victory. Then, they fly off toward the sunset. Jake and Maggie lift their glasses with pride, gesturing a sign of thanks to the whit-bits and clinking their well-charged glasses. Then, they sip their wine. All the while, their hearts are fluttering.

"This has been an exciting time for me, Jake. In some ways, I really think I am sorry to see this awesome adventure come to an end. I have felt, for the first time in my life, that I had a real sense of purpose beyond myself and my family. Damn it all anyway. It sure felt good doing something good for the betterment of our precious world."

"I hear you, Maggie. I, too, am sorry that our mission in life seems complete, as it will be difficult to top what we have just been through. So, perhaps a new puppy will fill the creative and demanding void we now face."

"I'm so glad that we decided to get a new puppy, Jake. I know that we have been extremely busy since Katey passed away, but it still doesn't feel the same when we get home. There is a real void or vacancy in our home. I miss the extra heart beat, the warm welcome, and just the comfort that she is always there wanting and willing to give whatever she can to make our lives more wholesome."

"Maggie, I agree with you, and I can tell you, even though puppies are a lot of frustrating work, I can't wait to pick her up tomorrow morning. Are you sure you want to call her Reese and not Snickers or Smarties?"

"Yes, Jake, I am sure she must be named Reese.

She is a beautiful, dark, strawberry blonde and has the will and the way that reminds me of that beautiful Hollywood actress Reese… Oh Jake, what exactly did you mean when you said our mission seems complete? What are you thinking?

"Our brains have not only developed in expanding our physical capabilities, but they also developed in a way that generates greater intellect from within. The edge that we have over the balance of our civilization is apodictic. This has not occurred so that we could simply enjoy a one-time event. It has occurred for other meaningful purposes. I believe our mission will resume soon; otherwise, we would not be here, but off in another world on another worldly mission, or we would be resting forever in Meadowbrook. We are here in the here and now, so our role in life is simply not complete."

"You know, Jake, I, too, have been having similar thoughts, and yes, we are not finished our mission in life just yet! Perhaps, we can play a major role in…"

"The New We? Hmm, you might be right, Babe."

"Jake, I wonder what ever happened to the Dalai Lama."

218

ABOUT THE AUTHOR

Making my debut in October 1947, with a little help from two wonderful parents in Vancouver, British Columbia, Canada, life has been, as expected, exceptional, and interesting.

While writing has always been in the back of my mind, in January 2006, I witnessed an oscillating, green vog with reverent mysticism near Parkers Ranch on the Big Island of Hawaii, and awe inspired me to write this book, *For the Good of All.*

I currently live in South Surrey/White Rock, British Columbia, with my lovely wife Margaret and our most prized golden retriever Reese, and we enjoy life as life should be in our paradise.

We are blessed with wonderful children and many gifted, delightful grandchildren.

LaVergne, TN USA
13 February 2010
172975LV00004B/3/P